A Chaser
On The Rocks

Simon Maltman

Solstice Publishing - www.solsticepublishing.com

A Chaser on the Rocks
A Novel by Simon Maltman

<u>Dedication</u>

For the three beautiful girls I live with (1 wife, 2 daughters)
and I suppose the cat called Syd too.

Chapter One

I arrived at The Causeway Hotel in the late part of the afternoon, drenched. It was a short walk from the tram, but long enough for the Antrim rain to beat any heat out of me. The Hotel was a chunky, oddly curved building overlooking the Giant's Causeway. It was a Wednesday in April 1941 and it was already getting dark. Northern Ireland never cared much for the seasons. I ducked in the front door, my suitcase dragging close behind, entered, and pulled off my hat. I glanced around, taking in a grand, panelled reception area and an ornate staircase. I padded over to the desk and to a mean-eyed old lady.

"Hello, the name's Chapman. I've got a room booked from today."

She looked to be getting meaner and, with some apparent effort, she pulled open a registration book. She examined it - appearing to hope I had the wrong place. I looked down at it too, over her thinning hair - rusted to her head. She shot me a look and returned to her search. I straightened up and looked around me with a shrug. There was a cosy, snug bar with a fire just started and a separate dining room not opened for dinner yet.

"Your key," she said, sourly.

She held it out, defeated.

"Many thanks," I said. "You've been most helpful."

She stared at me unendingly until I shivered and turned to walk down the hall. I checked the key - 109. No bellboy in sight or welcoming committee either. I started up the stairs.

"Mr. Chapman?" said a flustered voice from behind me.

I turned. "Yes?" I said, starting to feel tired after the long train, and tram journeys, from Belfast.

A rotund man in his early fifties trundled towards me, his cigar dropping ash on the floor and his torso perspiring a little through his striped shirt. He held out his hand, we shook.

"Mr. Chapman I'm terribly sorry I missed your arrival. I hoped to pick you up from the tram."

"That's okay; it'll save me bathing later. You're Mr. Loach?"

"Yes. I hope Maggie wasn't too... err well..."

"She's a treasure," *I winked. He smiled awkwardly, coming up another step towards me.*

"I'm afraid she's taken the recent news rather badly - she's not usually so..."

"Animated?" *I suggested.*

"Indeed."

We stepped to the side as a couple in their twenties ascended the stairs with a young baby in tow. I looked up the staircase after them. The hotel was really quite a grand old dame, she just needed a bit of makeup.

"Allow me to help you to your room, Mr. Chapman and then perhaps we can have a little chat."

"Thank you, but if it's all the same I'll just go up myself and change my clothes first. Can I meet you in the bar - say half an hour?"

"Whatever is convenient for you? Please ring down to the desk if there is anything you require. Take your time"

"Thanks. I might just call Maggie for a chat."

Chapter Two

"Not friggen bad," I meant to say only to myself. I looked up and the librarian raised her head above the parapet. She looked down again; mustn't have heard me properly. I glanced around the newly, white coated walls and let out a yawn. I noticed my laptop was nearly out of charge and leaned over and plugged it into the socket under the desk.

Chapter Three

I walked around the room as I stripped off my wet clothes. A large bed, desk, sink - everything I needed. Sitting on the bed in my underwear, I lit a cigarette. I breathed in deeply. The décor was pleasant enough but I couldn't have cared less if it was bare. This could have been up on the moon compared to the city. The Blitz had taken its toll on Belfast and a little on me. I was there to work but any respite, from where I had just come from, would be a holiday. It was only then I noticed the view. I had an enviable aspect over the Causeway - from the "Giant's Boot" to the "Giant's Pipe organ." Legend has it that the local giant - Finn McCool built a Causeway to get to Scotland and he left some of his bits and pieces lying around. I finished my smoke, changed my clothes, and felt just about human again. I hit the stairs inside the hour and went down to meet Loach. The first I had spoken to him was two days before when he had rung my office in Belfast. I don't stand on ceremonies like having a secretary, or getting much business for that matter, and had answered it myself. He told me how he was the owner of the hotel and that he was looking for the services of a private detective. He would put me up for free and cover my usual £4 a week. A fellow by the name of Frank McKenzie had been a walking tour guide employed by the hotel. He had died a few days earlier - his body found down by the rocks at the edge of the Causeway. He appeared to have tripped and fallen from one of the sheer cliffs above. The police apparently weren't much interested in investigating it thoroughly, but others were sure there had been foul play involved. I had nothing better to do so it seemed like a good job to take on. If the police felt they had bigger, and more international, fish to fry, I still had enough humanity to take the case.

Chapter Four

I clicked save and got out a Crunchie. Taking a bite, I thought about what I had down so far. I was pretty pleased. I had written the first paragraphs a few weeks before and was doing a bit of editing while I was in the library. It was going well but I was a bit worried I was ripping the shite out of Raymond Chandler. I noticed I was drumming on the desk a little bit. I had probably been doing it for a while; it used to piss my ex-wife off to no end. The librarian had slinked off some place leaving only a few kids in school uniform left to annoy. It had been some time since I had been this upbeat. I thought I'd educate them with some John Bonham style drum rolls. It was a good day and they seemed few and far between. I pulled out a bottle of water from my bag and took a long cool sip. "Real Irish spring" apparently. Well, it had been originally, perhaps, but I'd been topping it up from my kitchen in East Belfast for a couple of weeks. It may have been sucked straight out of the Lagan for all I cared; it tasted cool and refreshing to me anyhow. I checked I had enough smokes to last me a few hours and settled back down to write.

Chapter Five

I sat myself at the bar, lit a cigarette, and started on a pint of stout. Loach was instructing a waiter in the hall about something and when he saw me, he came straight across.

"I trust you found your room satisfactory Mr. Chapman?" he asked, eagerly.

"Yes, thanks. I hope Finn doesn't come back for his bed."

He looked blank for a second.

"Ahhh, yes I see, quite. Can I get you another?"

"Why not? I'll be a local and take a Bush."

He ordered us two Bushmills and ice and we decamped to a quiet booth. The ice made it sweetly cool. We got straight down to business, talking about the case.

"And you say he had no family?" I asked.

"No wife and children, both parents dead. Just a cousin who's a teacher at the wee school across the way - name of Mary McKenzie."

He took a slug from his drink and I got out another smoke.

"So what is it that makes you suspect foul play exactly?" I pressed.

"Frank knew this place like he knew his reflection. He could tell you how many blades of grass and the number of stones on the Causeway - you know? He was pushing fifty, but very fit and active. He'd lived around these parts all his life - same as me. He'd been doing the tours nearly ten years now. The police say he must have just slipped while out walking in the evening. But the cliff above had been sectioned off and he knew that because the path was eroding there for a long time...," he paused and sipped his drink. "He wouldn't have walked out that part.

Another thing is, these last few weeks, he wasn't himself. He wouldn't tell me anything but I know there was something very wrong."

He looked pained. I felt sorry for him. I felt sorry for Frank too - whatever happened to him. These were 'honest-to-God' type people up here with good hearts. Loach wanted to know what had happened to his friend and I could understand that. It didn't matter how many people were dying in those days - it would never be a case of just one more. Not for these people, anyway, and not for me. His eyes were glazed and he finished his drink. He signalled to the barman for another brace. His face was getting ruddier.

"What did Frank do before the walking tours?" I asked.

"He worked up at the distillery for about fifteen years - got sick of it, I think. He started out on the floor then progressed up to the middle offices."

"But there's no one about that you would call an enemy?"

"Nope. Everyone loved Frank. Everybody knew him, too. When you're a walking tour guide up here, you become part of the myth. They all get nicknames. Frank's was 'Finn's Chaser'. He was a real gentle giant that was Frank."

We had a couple more drinks and Loach had to go look after his business; for a start, there was something about a chef called Rory who had drunk a bit too much of an ingredient for his white wine sauce. I had my dinner in the dining room. I got the meat sweats on my brow and couldn't even finish my vat of vegetables. Rationing seemed not to apply here and I wasn't complaining. When I got to my room, the liquor had worn off but I was intoxicated with meat. I fell into a deep sleep. It was a good sleep, though I dreamt of giant cows.

Chapter Six

After an hour or so, I got up and went for a leak. I eyed my laptop with some concern as I walked quickly towards the toilets. It wasn't because I was busting but there could be wee, thieving shits about although this was fairly posh Bangor; those kids at the back of the room sharing an iPod for a start. They were doubtless, listening to some shit rap music. On my way back from the bogs, I could see my laptop safely sitting as I had left it. I eased to a normal walking pace and looked about me. I hadn't been to the old Carnegie Library in years. It had been refurbished with a huge, glass annex overlooking both Ward Park River and the old artillery gun beside the Remembrance epitaph. I looked out towards it and bought a coffee from the pod machine. It took me a minute or so to work out how to use the bloody thing. Once I had nailed the theory, I went about choosing the right pod. Whatever looked fucking strongest was my measuring stick. It worked okay and I had a steaming cup of coffee ready to drink. I'd seen a few people with these gadgets in their homes; I suppose they were trendy, would go along with hipsters and their fashionable beards. Then, you've got those who buy the coffee bags - another supposed innovation. There's a reason that teabags are the norm and coffee bags are not. It's cause they're shit. I don't understand why folk want to invent the wheel. Get a peculator and some coffee and give yourself three minutes; it's not rocket science. I sidestepped a few times to look into the study room to keep an eye on my stuff. I thought about my Great Uncle Victor and wondered if I could work him into the story somehow. He had been a pilot during the war. I wasn't really sure where the story was heading to but that was half the fun, I suppose. I hadn't tried any writing since university.

"It'll help you reconnect with your past. Write what you know and just enjoy it. I've worked with several ex-services and it really helped them." That's what my therapist had said, and I thought he was full of shit. I decided to give it a go anyhow. Since doing English Literature, and Modern History, at Queens in the nineties I had joined and left the RUC police force and finally lost my virginity. They were unconnected.

Chapter Seven

I went down to the dining room again for breakfast, at about nine-thirty in the morning, after a quick bath, shave and change of clothes. The Ulster Fry all but destroyed me with my stomach still recovering from the Olympic eating the night before. I sat in the resident's lounge for a little while. The wireless was on and it was more of the same in the news reports; bad bombings the night before, in particular, over London. Vivaldi was on as a nice Baroque filling between a stale sandwich of depressing news reports. Belfast was hanging in there. It was a dark time. There was a tangible discontentment across Belfast's community. And it really was that more than ever: one community. Protestants and Catholics still had their war but it would have to wait a while. Everyone was under attack together. North and South had been partitioned by an invisible curtain for a few decades and everything was still settling down. The last thing the South wanted in fairness was more bloodshed. The paramilitaries mostly went quiet too. A few years after the war, Carol Reed made Odd Man Out in post war Belfast and everyone wanted to be in the IRA again. A few years after that he made The Third Man and they all wanted a Zither.

Chapter Eight

Maybe he could fly over as Billy comes back to Belfast, I thought to myself. Victor apparently had a habit of flying his Spitfire low, over East Belfast, following the path of the river Conn. He freaked everyone out and got in a bit of bother for it. He never got to do it again after his plane went missing shortly after The Battle of Britain. I remembered my new, fancy coffee and reached around the stand for some mini milk cartons. None left, for fucksake. I walked back into the study room, glanced at my things and walked over to the desk. The librarian didn't look up and continued to finish typing whatever she was writing on the desktop computer. I waited patiently, though with some mild irritation, as the steam off my coffee reduced to a thin wisp. She glanced up very briefly and then looked down again, no 'Just a second' or 'I'll be right with you.' She was probably in her sixties, grey hair ponytailed, a tartan dress once popular around 1983 and about ten year's stubble on her chin.

"Excuse me," I said, finally, well after about ten seconds, but still.

I had, maybe, been a little louder than intended and she looked up with a jolt. She composed herself,

"I'll be right with you," she offered.

Fucks sake.

"Okay, thanks," I replied, trying to sound reasonable.

"Right, how can I help you," she asked, seconds later, professionalism personified.

"Can I get some milk please, there's none left on the stand?"

"Oh yes," she said, taking off her glasses from her bony nose. "I'm afraid we're all out."

"Well, could I get some please?"

"No, we do not have any, that is what I am saying," she said, with some irritation.

"I need a dash, I can't drink it without. Do you have some in your kitchen?"

"No, no we can't serve that to the public," she replied, with a haughty smile. "It wouldn't be allowed. I'm sorry, you will have to have it black."

"I don't drink it black," I said, shaking my head, "Right, just give me my money back please."

A few kids and other visitors had glanced over and the librarian lowered her tone,

"I'm afraid we cannot do that, it is a separate company who operates the machine."

"Frigs sake love, it's in your building, I just want my two quid."

"I'm afraid I cannot give that to you."

I sucked in my breath and said nothing more. I think it was personal growth. I left the coffee on the desk and stomped off, thirsty. I packed up my things in my rucksack and went out for a smoke. It calmed me down and my being pissed off at a little Hitler, uncompromising as she ran God's waiting room. I felt like a bit of a loner and I suppose I am one anyway. I stood at the side of the annex beside the playpark in Ward Park, toddlers screamed because they thought it was too early to go home and parents screamed back that it wasn't. Three ducks walked past me and then plonked into the river. A mother yanked a child in a trike, towards the edge, and tossed a few Pringles in for the birds. Lucky them. It was mild and dry out, and not even one of those "good days for ducks." I noticed one youngish mother with short, peroxide hair eyeing me, but not in a good way. She pulled up a young boy of three or four onto her shoulder and strode purposely towards me, despite the heels.

"Why are you staring at a children's park? Do you think that's okay?" she spat at me.

I was literally taken aback and bumped against the wall.

"What the fuck?" is all I could muster, less than tactfully.

"If you've got no kids you shouldn't be hanging outside a bloody playpark," she continued glancing at her kid. "And don't you curse in front of the child."

"Listen, love away, and fuck," I said, quieter. "It's no business of yours but I've been using the buckin' library."

"Well, then, get back in there or I'm calling the police and see what they think," she carried on.

"Jesus, your husband's a lucky fella."

"I'm not married you cheeky bastard but he'd still come down here and knock your shit in. Send you back in little pieces to your missus you wanker."

"Knock yourself out, she's dead anyway."

That slowed her down a little and she considered me closely.

"Well, look I'm sorry if that's true but...."

"*If* it's true?" I shouted. "What the fuck?"

I admit I lost it. I've got some issues but I'm usually not one to scream at women in playparks and make their children cry. Yes, the child sobbed as if someone had told them Santa had just been kneecapped and wouldn't be making it down any chimneys this year because he's on DLA.

"Now look what you've done! I won't tell you again. Fuck away off!" she said, and turned to walk away.

The blood pulsed in my neck and my palms were icy. I started forward to clear my head and startled her, making here stumble a little with the child.

"Get away from me!" she warned.

"I'm not going to touch you, you silly bitch. Yes, my wife is dead and now I won't be having any kids. So, I'm out here just having a fag and it's none of your fucking business anyway."

She calmed slightly and looked uncomfortable as more people, every second, twigged that something was happening and stopped and stared.

She flicked her hair and held the child close. "Well, you could still be a paedophile even if she is dead."

For some reason that didn't make me angrier and I slotted into a mode of controlled rage.

"Stop saying *if*. And even a nonce wouldn't go near you two. Your kid's a dog," I said, quietly but firmly.

Chapter Nine

It was a calm and sunny morning in Antrim, all rained out from the previous day. I drained my coffee pot and walked on outside. It was good coffee and that was harder to get in Belfast. I had never been to the Giant's Causeway before. Its reputation as a Wonder of the World is justified. I ambled down the steep incline towards the actual Causeway rocks. They are surrounded by steep cliffs and sprawling scenery. Along with a couple of 'Luckies', the scenery took my breath away. Climbing up the natural wall, I idled along to the Causeway's edge, letting the sea lap up against my shoes. I stood facing the sea looking out towards the Mull of Kintyre for a while. Then, I went back on myself and up to the cliffs. I soon located the place where McKenzie must have fallen from. The path was in fairly, bad shape. I walked to the steps, weaving down the cliff, and descended gingerly. I was pooped. There were three wreaths lying at the foot of the cliff. One from his cousin, one from the hotel and one from the distillery. I wandered around for another half hour and headed back towards the hotel. When I made it near to the top of the path again, I could see a forty-something man, around six foot with short, brown hair staring down at me. He was in a police uniform. As I got closer, he lifted out tobacco and papers and made up a smoke, not taking his eyes off me for a second. He looked the epitome of self-importance in a community still outside the bloodshed of war.

"You Chapman?" he asked, succinctly.

"Me Chapman - you Tarzan?" I asked, stopping in front of him. He looked suitably unimpressed.

"I'm Captain Robinson," he advised, in a clipped tone. He looked away for the first time and lit his cigarette with a gold-plated lighter.

"There is no need for any shoe flies coming up to my jurisdiction. Firstly, there's been no crime committed here. Secondly, I want you gone by the end of the day."

I took out a smoke, slowly, from my inside pocket and then met his stare. I lit up and breathed out. This guy had never seen a battlefield; even if he did think he was the local sheriff keeping out the Indians.

"I thought this was a nice, friendly tourist place. I haven't been exactly overwhelmed by Irish hospitality so far. I'll tell you what I'll do. First, I'm gonna finish my smoke. Second, I'm gonna stay here for as long as I damn well please."

He straightened up his back and tilted his head. "Now, you look here you jumped up, little hallion. I could have you whipped out of here and down the station before...."

"Let me stop you there Captain," I interrupted, "you've got squat on me and Nazis aren't in charge here. So, get out of my way."

I went to brush past him when he hit me with a quick right hook to my jaw. I wasn't expecting it and I went straight down into the grass. It didn't really hurt and I jumped right back up. He looked hungry for a brawl. I controlled myself. I could have, maybe, taken him but it wouldn't have been worth it.

"I'm tired Captain. Go and beat on your wife or something."

I walked on by this time without injury. He looked like I'd slapped him across the face with a kipper.

I headed directly to the bar. I was their only customer.

"Gimme a sherry, please."

The barman set it up and I paid him. Sometimes there's nothing tastier than a dry sherry. I felt the anger slowly drain away. I was determined to stay at least until the end of the week now, whether I found anything out or not. I'd happily work for free. Loach drifted in shortly afterwards, doing his rounds through the hotel. I told him about my chat with Robinson and he shared that he wasn't very popular with many of the locals either and told me not to worry about him. He was a control freak and thought he owned the place. Loach went on with his rounds and I took another sherry. I checked the timetables with my good chum Maggie at reception and took a bus into Bushmills village.

Chapter Ten

"Jesus, where did that come from?" I thought, feeling somewhat sheepish. Although not that many people had noticed, I still felt like Malcolm X at a Clan meeting as I sat down in the sofa area and pretended to read a copy of *The Sun*. There was a nice pair of tits on page three. It hadn't hurt as much this time talking about 'her'. Five years of therapy must have done some good. It was better than friends staring awkwardly at the floor and clearing their throats if I mentioned anything about the car bomb. I understood. "Bad luck" they all said. That's all they could say and how fucking sorry they were for me. I stared out towards the park and didn't give a shit what anyone thought, but felt a familiar flutter of anxiety. I thought about popping one of my Lorrazees for the first time in days. My current balance of Tegretol and Amisuplpride had been chemically evening me out up to that point. I took a few breaths of air outside instead and then had a bottle of full, fat Coke. I went back inside and up to the second floor. That was where they kept their World War II collection and why I was there in the first place. I washed my face and hands in the bathroom, and considered my reflection on the way out. I didn't look too bad for a man in his forties who drank, smoked, and had encountered a fair amount of bad luck. I went on up the staircase complimenting myself on how I'd not yet got any greys. Some of my mates were bald as fucking coots and had been for about twenty years already. I was no oil painting but it could have been worse. I had soaked up as many facts as I could from the Linen Hall Library in Belfast and had got the train the twelve miles to Bangor that morning. Over the previous two weeks, I had visited most of the libraries in

Belfast and North Down. I didn't plan for any bugger to ever read my story but I wanted to make it as good as possible. I don't really know why. I certainly wasn't going to tell my therapist about it - the smug twat. I was also enjoying seeing a bit more of the country for a change as well: especially since the Democratic Unionist Party had come back into office in East Belfast. The Catholics, gays and well informed were all fucked. It had been years since I had even visited one library, never mind a tour round nearly all of them. I hadn't been working a day job much and spending my time going to different wee towns was, well I suppose, quite fun. Donaghadee, Lisburn, Holywood, had all been visited over the previous week. It reminded me of University and I had always enjoyed the research aspect of assignments. In the Police Service Northern Ireland too, the paperwork was what most would always complain about, but it didn't bother me. The best collection had probably been in Lisburn but Donaghadee had the best Guinness. It also had, allegedly, the oldest pub in Ireland. Ireland has as many oldest pubs as it's had civil wars.

Chapter Eleven

Bushmills has always been a quiet place. The name is known worldwide, but this is just a small, unassuming village. I got off the bus and walked past a few school kids sharing a cigarette. They eyed me, suspiciously. I smoked a cigarette, too, as I went on by the few shops; a butchers, a grocers, no candlestick maker. It was a cold, dry day. I pulled my coat close to me against the North Antrim wind. It was a short walk up to the distillery and, as I approached it, there was a hustle of activity. Trucks arrived, just in front of me, leaving off essential ingredients and a large lorry struggled past with enough produce to keep me happily drunk for the rest of my life. The distillery dates back to 1608 but, of course, the buildings are a little newer than that. Well, most of them. A huge, factory tower dominated the skyline and there were many large, Victorian buildings surrounding it. Some were old, red, brick factory buildings steeped in whiskey and history. It looked like a nice place to work in but, for me, it would be like a diabetic working in a cake shop. I stopped at the gate and looked at a worker in cap and overalls, about ten yards the other side, smoking a badly made, rolled up cigarette. He threw it on the ground and came towards me. His eyes were deep set, he looked to be around forty-five, and he wouldn't be posing for many oil paintings.

"We're not open to visitors today," he half shouted, through the fence.

"I'm looking to speak to the boss," I said, flashing my private badge.

"Boss is away. You could come next week maybe?" he offered, generously.

"That's no good for me, I'll see someone else then."

He leaned against the gate attempting to look disinterested.

"That there's a private licence, so if I let you in I'm doing you a favour, okay?"

"Okay pal, whatever you say."

He gave me a final stare and then unlocked the bolts for the pedestrian entrance and pulled the gate across.

"I'll take you up to see Mr. Colrain," he said, and gestured for me to walk to the left. He probably expected a tip.

"I thought you might have wanted to ask why I'm here," I said.

He ignored me and shut the gate behind us.

The guy led me through the courtyard as if he was mute. I found out later he was called Ferguson and he was the Assistant Work-Force Manager. I looked around as we walked, thinking about all the money I'd donated to these fellas over the years. They owed me. Maybe a new liver. He took me through a room full of casks - floor to ceiling up fifty foot. I had a sudden pining for Belfast and wondered how the city was doing without me. It wasn't just the death that upset me during The Blitz, it was seeing my hometown destroyed. I had lived in East Belfast all my life and there's not much worse than seeing your boyhood football team's ground annihilated. Glentoran's ground. The Oval was left with a large crater in the middle of an unplayable pitch. Even Danny Blanchflower couldn't have dribbled around it. The Jerrys were looking to take out Harland and Wolff and to put a stop to the industrial contribution that Belfast was giving to the war effort. One hundred and eighty bombers visited Belfast that Easter Tuesday and it certainly quietened the city down. All contact was lost with a squad of Hurricanes tasked with protecting the city and the result was no German losses and, around, a thousand locals killed.

"Wait there," Ferguson said, finally.

I walked another step and smiled at him as I dug out a cigarette. He went over towards a group of three men huddled around a large group of crates. They were all in suits, gesturing and pointing; two of them with notebooks in their hands. The third man was dressed extra smartly. He looked to be in his forties with a hat and a moustache to keep him warm in the cool warehouse. He was thin with green eyes and I thought his smile was a little crooked. Ferguson took him to one side and they both glanced at me over the other men's shoulders. The man with the moustache then returned to his conversation with the other men in suits. I finished my smoke and watched Ferguson as he came back towards me.

"I'll take you to his office. He'll be up shortly," he said.

Ferguson left me in Colrain's office, offering no more of his jovialities. It was big, bold and, well, very gaudy. There was a nice view of the surrounding countryside and you could almost see all the way out to the stones. I liked the panelled walls and the leather furniture. I didn't like the brash, "artsy" photographs on the walls or the eastern looking ornaments I'm sure someone else had picked out for him.

"Mr. Chapman," Colrain boomed, with an outstretched hand. "How do you like my office?"

I shook his hand.

"Not really what I'm used to. More an East Belfast man than East Asia."

He didn't know what to make of that and squinted slightly, gesturing for me to sit. I sat down on a grand suede chair and he sprawled out slightly on a maroon leather sofa.

"Can I offer you a wee dram?"

His voice still contained a North Antrim lilt, but had been refined a little more hops now than barley.

"Thank you, I take an occasional sniff."

He fetched us both a large one from a globe drinks cabinet in the corner and served each in a wide mouthed glass. He sat back down.

"This is our reserve. I think you'll like it. You'll forgive me for not offering ice or water, I can't abide seeing it sullied."

"That's fine with me, I like it neat."

He took a slow gulp and changed position.

"What can I do for you, Mr. Chapman?"

"It's about Frank McKenzie."

I waited for a reaction, but there was none.

"I'm looking into his death, it was very sudden and there was some strangeness surrounding it."

"Yes, yes, it was very sad. I didn't know him very well, unfortunately. I had been out of the country for much of the time he was here. I was working on overseas trade."

He spoke fairly flatly and then looked a little too eager.

"Strangeness, you say Mr. Chapman, what do you mean by that exactly?" he asked.

I took my first sip of the drink and let his question linger for a few seconds.

"That really is good. A fine blend," *I paused.* "Yes, strangeness. Mr. McKenzie was a very, experienced guide who knew the rocks well. He fell from a place that was closed off and long after working hours."

"Yes uh huh," *said, Colrain thoughtfully.* "But not that strange, really, knowing the weather here and the sudden deterioration of the cliffs at times."

"There are people who think it strange enough," *I offered, bluntly and lit up an accompaniment for my whiskey.* "Can you tell me much about his time working here?"

Colrain looked slightly pained and then breezier again.

"As I said, I did not know the man in any meaningful capacity, however I do know he was well-liked and was a good worker. He did very well for himself here, too, a fine man by all accounts."

"Yes, I was wondering about that. If he had worked his way up to the offices, he must have been on a good wage. What would make him pack it in and work for chips as a tour guide?"

"I'm afraid you would have had to have asked him that. I don't know, too much pressure perhaps, desire for the outdoors?"

"Perhaps," I said, blowing out a little smoke. "Who would know better? Did he leave on good terms?"

"My superior would know better than me, I would think. Mr. Dufferin, the owner of the distillery. He knew Frank quite well, I understand. I'm afraid he is away on business at present and I do not know when to expect him. He is working out of our Dublin office for at least the rest of the month. Transportation problems and such because of the war. I'm sure you can imagine."

He got to his feet, indicating our conversation was ending. I necked the rest of my drink and then rose.

"Thanks for your time, Mr. Colrain, you've been very helpful," I lied.

"Not at all, I hope you enjoyed your visit and sorry I couldn't be more informative."

"I had a bad taste in my mouth when I came in, but it's nicer now."

He didn't know how to take that either.

Chapter Twelve

Bangor Library was coming up trumps about the Belfast Blitz and the bombings down in Dublin. I hadn't known before starting my "masterpiece" that the Republic had been bombed in the war. My East Belfast education had omitted these "trivialities" relating to our friends across the border. The friggers should've joined in but still. Death was death. There was some other good material about rationing, blackouts and evacuations and I was glad I had gone there. I left about three and walked around to Bangor Castle. Don't get excited, it's not actually a castle, it's a bit like how Piccadilly Circus is bereft of clowns and acrobats. It's the old, stately home that the lords and ladies would have lived in and now the home of the council and a heritage centre. I was after the heritage part, but first I needed the café for two cups of coffee, both with the luxury of milk. I wandered around the centre, primarily there to view the exhibition about the war, but I looked around the whole place. They had done a good job for a free, local museum. There was an interesting section on the Viking raiders. A pillaging the good people of Bangor. Maybe I'd set my second novel with them, *A Viking on the Docks*? The last display I looked at was a mock up of Victorian Bangor, all seaside, gulls, buckets and spades and sweety rock. These days it would be more like dog shit, sewage and empty bottles of Buckfast. However, I did allow my cynical self a little reminisce. We used to visit Bangor when I was a child growing up in Belfast. It was the Amalfi coast of North Down. My childhood wasn't doom and gloom, it was just in my adulthood that things went pear shaped. Many a weekend we would go down to the beach, paddle our toes and have a poke on the sand (for those outside these six counties a poke means an ice cream with a flake). The museum closed at four-thirty and I stepped out into the outside to a gentle breeze and the easy laughter of kids finishing school, their lives without responsibility. I reflected on the productive day that I'd had so far with just the one altercation. *Didn't we have a lovely time the day we went to Bangor?*

High Street is the main area for Bangorians to get blitzed. It was still light, for March, when I got there and a few pasty locals were sitting in some of the front beer gardens. Or, should I say, squatting on shitty benches beside an ash bucket. A few "gardens" had an Ikea, pot plant too. Bangorians really think they are something. But really it's just a stupid wee town with as many buck-eeijits and arseholes as anywhere else. So they have Pickie Park and stupid, wee, plastic swans that parents can pay eight quid for a ride on. *They have an old, Victorian Manor and an Olympic swimming pool, but who really gives a shit?* It's a poor man's Blackpool and everyone there drives a bloody Volvo. Despite that, I was soon in Donegans's back beer garden enjoying a pint of Smithwicks and treating myself to a Henry Winterman. The beer garden was actually nice and there were a few groups filling out the picnic tables and chairs. The back fence was high and covered in ivy, making the place feel pleasantly enclosed. By July, it would be heaving. Everyone seems to drink in July. That, and everyone buys tennis rackets after fancying themselves as pros thanks to Wimbledon.

"Any good music on tonight, mate?" I asked, of a man a bit older than me, smoking a Menthol with his vodka and Red Bull.

He mumbled something disinterestedly consisting most helpfully of 'dunno.' Maybe I was best sticking to my own company today I decided.

Chapter Thirteen

When I got back to the hotel I had just beaten another, huge shower and felt great satisfaction in my timing. I rewarded myself with another whiskey and an hour's nap. I had a shower and went down to the dining room for about seven. The rain outside had faded out and then came back with a vengeance and turned into an Irish monsoon. I took another sip of my bottle of stout and decided the visit I planned to Mary McKenzie could wait until the morning. I ordered a steak, again, despite the sweats from the night before, but skipped the starter and dessert. I had a few cups of coffee after my meal and Loach joined me for a quick brandy. He looked a bit disappointed that I had little to tell him, but he didn't say anything about it. I padded round to the resident's lounge afterwards, by myself, and sat in a corner snug, moving onto shorts. For a while, my mind drifted to the war and my part in it. I had joined up a little before the war started and last served almost a year to the day to when I was sitting in that bar. The last action I had was at The Battle of Boulogne and I was part of the Irish Guards who were defending the town and port. We fought like warriors, but were overrun by the Krauts, eventually. It wasn't a long wait until the evacuations at Dunkirk and I didn't have to go back again. It might have been different if the draft had spread to Northern Ireland. I don't mind saying that the thought of seeing those Panzers still makes me feel sick with a terrible dread.

Chapter Fourteen

I ate a cheesy beano on the way up to the eleven o'clock train. I was two sheets to the wind and the hill on Main Street heading up from the Marina was hard work. I stopped halfway and looked down towards the piers. The McKee clock stands tall, overlooking the three piers behind the town centre. It doesn't really stand tall as it's about twenty foot, let's just say "it stands." Main Street was quiet, as all the shops were closed, and High Street was where the majority of pubs are. I remembered the old C&A department store long before the new mall was built over it. I also remembered coming to Bangor on two less happy occasions; when on duty. Bangor was bombed twice during the Troubles and Main Street was ripped up by it. Fortunately no one was killed. A mate of mine worked in the bar up Bingham Mall and had been asked to go and put the shutter up on the alleyway as there was yet another bomb scare. He had gone up whistling and started to pull it down just as the blast went off outside. He had the shutter just below his face when the bomb blew him up to the other end. Lucky bastard practically got straight up and walked away.

I didn't have another smoke until I got to Dufferin Avenue, the street next to the station and the scourge of Bangor's Chamber of Commerce. Known as "Sufferin'" Avenue by the locals, it houses a concentration of the population's drunks, druggies, hookers and Christians. That's two Gospel Halls, a brothel, one Homeless hostel and a solicitors'. I walked past the second hand bookshop there too. It was closed.

"Ellroy's are very collectable, nobody wants to part with them," the owner had told me earlier that day. "They love these original covers too," the older man had added, leaning his wiry frame against the counter.

"It's the same with vinyl," I said.

"It's the smell of the book," he said, holding it up like a Maltese Falcon. "The feel of the pages and the artwork too."

"That's what gets me about records. A nice hundred eighty gram vinyl, especially in a gatefold or with coloured sides."

"I still have a fondness for cassettes too. They were a revelation in their day," he said, and lost me. I'm an analogue fan for records and reel-to-reel recording but tapes are terrible. They were a pointless invention. You couldn't skip to songs and the sound quality sucked. I suppose mix tapes were quite good.

***

I stayed awake on the train despite the several shots and few chasers I had consumed during the evening. Looking out the window, I watched the countryside whizz past and I thought about Antrim. I'd have to take a trip again to re-acquaint myself with the place properly. I hadn't been there since my parents had both been alive. But that would all have to wait because I had to see a client in the morning. It was the first case I had taken on that year. It would be fair to say I hadn't been enjoying great, mental health and my PI career hadn't exactly taken off. When I got to Sydenham, I walked onto the platform and on up towards my place on the Newtownards Road. The Harland and Wolfe cranes greeted me, the yellow painted metal cutting through the evening mist. The Titanic was built over there. *She was alright when she left here* is the slogan but frig me what other country celebrates a great big fuck up like that? I felt really hungry for a new case the next day despite the chips. I didn't plan on taking anything too adventurous on anytime soon but it didn't quite work out that way. That night I woke up in the early hours, my room felt freezing. I still felt drunk and my head was sore. The room was almost pitch black, but my vision began to distort and I could feel a migraine starting. There was no point in staying awake. I wrapped the covers in a tight net around me and reached out for sleep.

Chapter Fifteen

I took in the room and put the war to the side. I talked myself into feeling better. I had a new case to think about. The rain had stopped outside and the moon lit up the Antrim hills. I was feeling a nice glow when she walked in.

"I'm sorry, are you Billy?"

She took down her hood and her lightly dampened, auburn hair fell to one side. She looked me in the eye apologetically.

I stood up.

"Yes, hello," I said, and it was all I could utter. She wasn't movie star, glamour-beautiful, but she was a beauty in anyone's book. I gestured for her to sit and she removed her damp raincoat. She looked slender in her cream dress and a little incongruous amidst the rest of us ordinary looking folk. She held out an elegant, milky hand.

"I'm sorry to barge in on you, my name is Mary."

She smiled and I shook her hand.

"Nice to meet you, you're Frank's cousin?"

There was a flicker of sadness. "Second cousin, yes."

"I cared for him very much," she paused.

"Can I get you a drink?" I ventured.

"If I'm not intruding, yes, thank you."

I started to feel more comfortable; maybe it was the thought of another drink to settle me down. I lit us both a cigarette. The circumstances were against us but we were at ease in each other's company. Maybe in a different place, at a different time, something could have happened. She was warm and gentle and I hadn't felt so engaged by anyone for a long time. She only told me everything I had already gotten from Loach but I didn't mind listening to it again the way she told it.

"Well, that is everything I wanted to say really, Mr. Chapman. I'm just so glad that you're doing something. I didn't think everything was quite right either and, at least now, I'll feel like something's been done; even if there aren't any answers. He was drinking more and he hadn't been himself," she stared out the window at the easing rain and said, quietly, *"It just wasn't right."*

I told her again that I, too, believed there was something more to it than just an accident and that I would be doing a full investigation. To be honest, I wasn't very sure there was much to discover.

"He seemed to just want to spend all his evenings on his boat recently," she said, wistfully staring out the window again. *"I don't think he had many real friends left. He was still adored by everyone, don't get me wrong, but I mean 'real' friends."*

We finished our third drink, after sitting for about an hour, and I promised her that I would do what I could. And, I meant it. We then chatted for a while longer and I almost forgot what I was there for. She said she'd wait for the rain to ease off and reached for the bar's newspaper.

"Are we going to discuss some local politics?" I asked.

"I only read them for the funnies," she answered.

"I like those too."

A few brave souls drifted out of the bar. Unfortunately, the rain wasn't long in passing.

"I'd better be getting back for my wee daughter," she said, reaching for her coat.

"Oh," I said, with genuine surprise, forgetting myself a little. I decided to test the waters. *"Your husband will be wondering where you are I'm sure."*

She slowed putting her coat on and looked me in the eye.

"I don't have a husband. I have a daughter called Evie who's with her Nan. Her Daddy was a serviceman and was killed in the war. He was stationed here for a while and we went to England to get married. I lived there for a time last year."

"Oh," I said, again. "I'm sorry to hear that. What unit was he in?"

She finished wrapping up and stood up briskly.

"He was an Englishman, Mr. Chapman, and was in the RAF. I'm sorry I really must go, it was nice to meet you." She gave me a farewell smile. Then she was gone.

***

I lit up a smoke and enjoyed the warmth of the bar and the hubbub. It was going on from eleven that night and I was only the slightest bit drunk. I decided to make the short walk round to The Nook bar, about a hundred yards away. That was where all the locals drank and that's where I could do a bit of my own archaeology. As I walked between bars, there were a few other scallywags going back and forth like on a merry-go-round for drunks. Captain Robinson was leaning against a gate, in the field, opposite about fifty yards away. I don't know if he was watching me as such, but he looked at me as I walked past, betraying no reaction.

Chapter Sixteen

My mind had come up with a few ideas for the love story a bit later on and drifted back to the coolness of my car and a desire for some nicotine. *Click... click* went the lighter again. I through it on the floor of the car and rummaged in my jacket pocket for another one. Nothing was in that pocket but some lint stuck to an old glacier mint. I tried another pocket, pausing to wipe my breath from the window again. The second pocket brought a little bit of satisfaction and I lit up my hand-rolled "Drum." I exhaled and looked closely at the house I had been watching. I was nervous having been caught up in my writing and had not prepared for this new case properly. There was more nothingness to watch after the previous two hours of nothing. I was bored, mostly. The private detective game hadn't been as glamorous as I may have imagined. Ten months of it and I almost wished I was back in the RUC again in the nineties. Almost. The house was in a fairly quiet, working class street in North Belfast. "Fairly quiet" as in no burned out vehicles or armoured car roadblocks. I finished my smoke. For dessert I had a packet of Minstrels and some full fat Coke. I took out my wallet and checked I had my ID in case any police did come by and wonder what I was up to. It was unlikely as there would be other things to be doing in Belfast that night I imagined. My *Brian Caskey- Private Investigator- Licence 2001, 675* was in its usual place.

***

I had been following this guy, on and off, for a couple of days. It was a jealous wife thing that wasn't paying much, but it covered my tobacco and confectionary and got me out of the house. This fella, by all accounts, was a bit of a hood according to his wife. She loved him but would merrily chop off his nuts if he was playing away. It was nearly ten at night and I was getting sleepy when the husband finally came out of the building with two other men. They disappeared into the garage before headlights went on and they all emerged again inside a white estate car. They eased past me a few doors down and I slumped in my seat. I waited until they had turned out into a trickle of traffic. "Shut up" I said, to the voice telling me to get a carryout and go home. For once it was talking sense. My eight-year-old Ford reluctantly wheezed to life. As I followed at a distance, the initial adrenaline eased and my mind began to wander towards the mundane. *Why do cars always push in from the third lane on the Sydenham bypass? Why did the Centra at Ardoyne not stock cans of full fat, fucking Coke?*

"Do you have a strategy when you're playing Monopoly?"

"How do you mean?" I asked.

"Like, I always go for the stations first and then aim for the big guns."

"Oh, I see. Yeah, just the utilities for me first and then I try and get a few blue or orange type monopolies."

"Fair play," the owner of Gallopers café had said, approvingly earlier that day. They did a nice "Ulster" there.

My mind flitted back as I realised I nearly didn't stop at a red light. I was getting a bit close to my quarry as well.

"You're losing it," the voice said.

My pulse increased a beat and I ignored it, grabbing the wheel tightly. I skilfully lifted a pre-rolled smoke off the dash, lit it and settled back in my seat. I'd take a tablet in a little bit, I thought to myself.

***

We journeyed on out to Mallusk and into the dreary, industrial estate there. My curiosity was given another shot in the arm and I breathed in smoke, heavily. We had passed most of the brightly, security-lit buildings, car dealers, cash and carries and furniture stores. They parked by a dark cul-de-sac, I switched off my lights and coasted just out of sight at the road before. After a protracted two minutes, the three slipped out, silently, all wearing dark jackets. They walked purposefully back up the road they had driven down, staying close to the wall. This all wasn't really in my remit but I popped one of my pills and got out of the car. I tailed them at a distance. When they disappeared around the front of the building I realised that we were at the side of the Metro-City Bank. It would be closed but the office lights on upstairs indicated that someone was working late. I hunched down on the ground around the front side of the perimeter. I remember feeling a fuzziness as I knelt.

***

I must have had an absence for a minute or two because I could hear some faint noise in the distance and realised that they had all disappeared from view. Reaching to check for my phone, I realised I had left it in the car and my smokes too. I started to idle back towards the car when I heard what sounded like a large door slam followed by fast footsteps. I jumped over the three foot, outer wall onto the grass at the side of the driveway. Ducking down behind it, my breath rattled in my throat and a wave of nausea splashed about my stomach. I felt cold, but clammy, in my jacket and pulled it close to me opening out my collar. The footsteps had turned the corner and were running towards me. Each pair sounded several paces behind the other. One set passed and I stiffened. An alarm started to scream out into the cold air. A second pair of trainers raced past. The last set approached and for no good reason my body shot up. I looked the husband in the eye before I lunged at his sprinting silhouette, pushing him over with a shove. I tumbled over the wall after him and scrambled to get up myself; a few feet to the side of him. A blaze of light danced on my eyes and half my vision melted away like a Dali clock. Two scuffled steps and he was on me. I flapped like a swan in a sand pit and hit out as best I could. We rolled and I could feel my back scraping on stones and dirt. He hit me a few more times but was too close to hurt me much. I heard shouts, then the beginning of car sirens as he started to try and get off me. I got in a punch to his back which I could hear in his groan had hurt him some. He seemed to struggle to his feet and this time the running was accompanied by a siren duet. I fell against the wall and felt unconsciousness almost overwhelm me. The sirens were close now and an engine started. There was a crash of metal on metal, then a car door and more shouting. I went to sleep.

***

A night in Casualty was followed by a week of police and local paper interviews. That was followed by a pat on the back from the mayor and a picture in one of the aforementioned papers. It was all a bit mad. This was followed by the receipt of a small, pay package from the bemused wife. Then, I had a brief feeling of contentment interrupted by a spell in a local, mental health institution; Knockbracken, and countless hours with psychologists and psychiatrists. Afterwards, there was a short holiday in Portrush that proved more depressing than Knockbracken was. I suppose you want to know a bit about Knockbracken. I had been detained in the "short stay" institution that I believe overlooked a beautiful, Victorian park. Not that I'd fucking know because there were only windows on one side and they were overlooking the car park. All I could see were the mustard buses and industrial bins. The day room was nice enough and all the staff were trained in being "person centred" and "anti-restrictive," but most of them I wouldn't have recruited as a paperboy. I'd met para-military sociopaths with better social skills. My room was bare and it stank of disinfected cleanliness. I wasn't even allowed my guitar; maybe they thought I'd do myself a mischief with the guitar strap. I didn't write much of my story for a few weeks and nothing when I was under a voluntary sanction. Weird, fucking "voluntary," when you're not allowed to leave. I was only there ten days anyway and then I felt back to normal. Well, I don't know if it was normal, but I felt like I usually did. They say that twelve percent of Northern Ireland's population have mental health problems connected to "The Troubles," so what's the norm?

"How are you feeling today Brian?" my mental health nurse Amanda had asked on my last day.

"The voices tell me that I should kill everyone," I answered, with a large smile.

Amanda did not smile. She scowled at me and crossed her legs. She was a frumpy girl in her early forties, all teeth and no room for tongue in cheek.

"I don't think that is very funny considering how unwell you have been."

"Well, they say humour is a great tonic. Okay, I'm sorry, I feel great and I appreciate all the help you've given me. I feel I'm ready to go home now."

I didn't really believe any of that, particularly the part about appreciating her help. She had been a pain from start to finish; patronising and insincere. Luckily, I was able to play her all the time as she wasn't very bright. I probably should have been there for a lot longer, but Amanda's unfaltering belief in her own abilities helped to get me sent home.

Like I said, I then took a wee trip up to Portrush. Frig knows what I was thinking. I suppose you could say Portrush is the Las Vegas of Northern Ireland. Maybe that's too much of a stretch. It was wet and miserable and I spent most of the time in a couple of bars and knocking around in tat shops. It didn't do much good for my mental health. I'm not into golf, so I didn't give a shit about the supposed "world class" golf courses either. Portrush is close to the Causeway, but I didn't go to see it. I'm not sure why. One thing was that I couldn't get motivated to write any more of my story. The thought of it was like washing the car or cleaning out the cupboards. I didn't really do much of anything come to think of it.

I stayed in the house a lot after the weekend in Portrush and didn't come out much at all for weeks. I didn't feel anxious or annoyed. That was the problem. I didn't feel anything but empty. I was on pretty heavy medication, too. What I did do, suddenly, was to write again night after night. Gradually, I rose out of the slump I was in. I was waiting on a decision by some suit in City Hall as to whether I could keep my PI licence and I didn't really want to think about it much. I didn't know where I, or Billy, were headed but it excited me.

***

"Come in Brian, good to see you."

I closed the classroom door and took a seat in the second row, keeping my head down.

"The story is really quite insignificant in a sense," Richard Catherwood continued. "The more important attribute should always be the character. It's the playing of the game that matters if you like. I've often found that the most interesting plots I've tried to write have also had the dullest characters. What does everyone think? Am I full of twaddle?" He smiled and gave an open gesture with both hands.

I took the opportunity to look around the room properly and to see who had turned up to the meeting. I had been going to the writer's group at Queen's for a couple of months, but not for the last few weeks with all the, well, craziness. I hadn't really done much socialising at all for a while. I had enjoyed being part of the group despite my initial protestations to my psychiatrist that I was sure I would loathe it. It was due to finish for the term in a few weeks and I wanted to get to the last sessions.

"I agree with you, but a character by themselves wouldn't make much of a novel," Frank chipped in, one of the six or seven in the room that night. It was a decent group of people that went and it varied from week to week. What I liked was that there was no one who was completely up their own arse. There were a few who I certainly was never going to be best buddies with, but that was fine.

"I hear what you're saying," Catherwood responded. "But let me challenge you a little. I would suggest that a really good character could make the most mundane come to life. In fact, good storytelling, I believe, can also make the ordinary vital and fascinating."

"So, what do you think is more important - character or style?" Amy asked, from the back.

"That's a difficult one. I would be hard pressed to choose, but what I would say is they are both more important than plot. Take *The Big Sleep*, nobody cares that Chandler forgot to tell us who killed the chauffer. Then there are Harvey Pekar's graphic novels. They are tremendous but sometimes the biggest plot development is him getting out of bed."

He should know, I thought to myself, Catherwood had produced a very successful series of spy novels and a second series of black comedies set in a political party office in Belfast.

We split into three groups after which was the bit I always dreaded but ended up enjoying. We were encouraged to talk about what we had been writing and just to share as much as we wanted. I was still a little bit under par and found it hard to get warmed up. Once everyone had shared, and I had made a few comments, I felt I could say something about my work.

"I've been doing some research on my character set in Belfast in the forties. He's a PI."

I stopped to see if anyone's facial expression displayed any ridicule. There wasn't.

"I've been going round all the local libraries and museums, found out a lot of good stuff."

"That sounds really interesting," Amy said, warmly. She looked like she was still a student, small with a round face and short black hair. There was a real mix in the room of old and young. I suppose I was somewhere in-between, neither side would want to claim me as their own.

"You might want to check out Belfast War Memorial," Adrian suggested, he was the rather rotund, spectacled Godfather of the group. I would guess a mature student. "It would surely provide you with a lot of facts and information."

"Thanks, I will."

I ended up being last out the door and hovered as Catherwood tidied his laptop into his bag.

"Well, Brian, how are you? We'd missed you for a couple of weeks." I noticed how tall and wiry he was for the first time, I think I'd heard he was in his early fifties, but he looked well on it.

"Yeah, sorry about that. I got tied up with a lot of work stuff. I enjoyed the session tonight."

"Good," he said, flicking shut the clasps on his briefcase "We have a nice little group here, some very talented writers."

He walked to the door and held it for me to go on through. "You must let me see some of your work sometime. A period piece isn't it?"

"It is, yeah. Maybe I'll bring a few chapters in sometime."

Chapter Seventeen

There was pain the next morning. I thought it would only go as far as my head and stomach that seemed to already have swapped places. My head churned and my stomach had a migraine. There was a knock on the door and I realised there was probably a preceding knock that had woken me from my drunken sleep. I wrenched open the stiff, clean linen and slid off the side. My head and stomach swapped back and my head started to throb in protest.

"Mr. Chapman, there is a call for you," the young bellhop said, after I heaved the door ajar.

"Could you take a message please?" I offered, squinting and double-checking I was wearing trousers.

"I'm afraid the manager said it is very urgent."

"OK, gimme a second please," I said, beaten.

I closed the door and sorted myself out a little. I ran my hand through my hair and grabbed my cigarettes.

"OK, thanks son," I said, and gave him a penny.

We set off down the hall and I spoke little, drifting over the thick, red carpet. I lit up a cigarette before we hit the grand staircase. It tasted bad. When I got to the bottom, Loach was ambling around the reception desk and ushered me behind it and into the office. He shut the door. The bellhop hopped.

"Have a seat, Mr. Chapman, please," he said, offering me a chair beside an off the hook receiver. I noticed a clock above it that said it was 09.15.

"What's this about?" I asked, slowly grinding my smoke into a tray.

"They just said it is some bad news I'm afraid. They want to talk to you. Please, take your time."

His eyes fixed on me, he shifted onto the balls of his feet, opened the door and left. I took a breath and reached out for the receiver.

***

The train seemed to take forever to come and then forever and a day to make the journey back to Belfast. In between stops I begrudged a few tears and smoked a few cigarettes. I even managed a short nap. I had a terrible thirst; thirstier than a desert camel after a double hump removal. I couldn't tell what was making my stomach hurt; the drink from the previous night or the news that my mother had passed away.

***

The train pulled into Great Victoria Street Station during the evening, close to curfew time. I noticed all the city smells more keenly; despite only having being away for a few days. The city was dark, cold, polluted and oppressive. It was haunted by more souls than the last time I was there. I was out of cigarettes and felt annoyed at my annoyance when there was so much more to be thinking about. As I walked, it started to drizzle and I headed to the bus stop near City Hall. There were fewer buildings there, but I couldn't have told you if they had gone that week or the last. The day continued to be dreamlike. I hardly knew how I had made it across the country. When I got the news I was in shock. I wasn't used to feeling so out of control. People were nice to me. Loach offered a warm pat on my shoulder and even Maggie had a flicker of concern across her wrinkly scowl. I told Loach that I would have to go right away and he said he understood. I think I said something about not being convinced that Frank had been killed. There might be a story or two worth uncovering, but nothing to suggest a murder. Despite my daze I managed to move fast and got packed up quickly. Loach offered to give me a lift in his motor to the bus stop. Unsurprisingly, it was raining again as we pulled up and I finished another cigarette. He tried to give me some payment but I refused. I kept thinking about Mary and the sadness she kept within her and how it pushed her on. I scribbled her a note and pressed it into Loach's hand. I explained, in a few lines, why I was leaving so suddenly and that I would contact her again. I wrote that I was sorry for her loss and that I thought it had been a tragic accident. I hoped my Mother hadn't suffered any either.

***

Belfast felt strange to me. The bus had left me off a few streets from my terrace in East Belfast. I was walking along Dee Street, near the wreckage of The Oval when the sirens started. I immediately thought of my mother the night before and how she would have heard a similar warning. She either hadn't been quick enough or her stubbornness had kept her from leaving home. A German bomber crew saw to leveling most of her street. I regretted not having any kind of meaningful relationship with her and that I had only laid eyes on her twice in recent months though she only lived a few miles from my home. Suddenly, I realised that I was running and a few other poor sods out after dark were running too. My blood cooled when I thought I could hear the faint hum of a large aircraft. I was half a mile from the closest shelter when the hum became a rumble, followed by a few, dull bangs. I was now the only person about and I could hardly see more than a few feet in front of me thanks to the shrouding of Belfast like a widow in mourning. Only a street away sounded the whiz of something flying through the air, falling away from the deep hum of aircraft engines. After a few anxious seconds, there was a deafening explosion. "Just run!" I shouted inside my head. I shouted it again, this time aloud and sprinted for the corner leading to the street with the shelter. For some strange reason, I pictured, vividly, a courtship I had had several years earlier. We were dancing in the Floral Hall in North Belfast, up on Cavehill. I had taken this girl to the zoo first and we had seen chimpanzees swinging and tigers being fed their lunch. Afterwards, we drank a little too much and danced all night in the Floral Hall. I could smell what it had been like. Different from the sulphur I smelt at that moment. I could remember walking up the steps to the art deco façade and lighting up a cigarette and one for the girl. I wondered if Mary McKenzie would have liked it there. I heard another explosion further away than before and felt some relief. I ran up the path to the shelter panting and sweating, cold beads all over my body. I threw myself upon the metal door, cranked it open and dove inside.

Chapter Eighteen

I was standing outside a dreary block of flats in North Belfast. It was right in the middle of the so called "sectarian interface" and it was hard to tell if it was closer to the side with the Jacks or the Tricolours. I walked briskly past some teenagers, kicking cans, smoking and generally looking clichéd. I went through the unlocked, front door and slowed a little, climbing the stairs. It stank. I had been watching the building from my car, for a couple of hours, after my quarry had gone in. A lot of dodgy looking people had come and gone. The suit in City Hall had grudgingly let me keep my licence and, after some new therapy, I had eventually got back to work. I just had to meet up, occasionally, with a social worker now too - Nicola something or other. Everything was back in place. I had missed the work. It scared me to death at times, but I needed it. I was on a case paid for by a disgruntled, pub landlord. He had been victim to a large theft of drink and didn't want to go to the police nor the thugs he was paying "protection" to. I popped a pill and lit up a cigarette. The halls were quiet for around eleven o'clock at night, in a dilapidated block of flats, in this part of town. I checked again that I had my PI badge in the inside pocket next to my lighter.

***

It had been a slow enough two weeks tracking down this particular nineteen year old to this particular block of flats. I had been up and down Belfast after a few dead ends, but I was sure I had found one of the liquor thieves. He would probably be ignoring the cases of fine malt and, instead, be necking a few litres of Bucky or so I thought. When I got to the flat, the door was ajar and I gave it a light tap. I looked around me, first, before stepping through. Inside there was a dim light illuminating the dirty walls and the sparse interior of the rank bed. It was humming. There was an uneasy tension in the air but I felt quite calm. It could have been because I sensed whatever had happened had past, or that my medication had kicked in. As I moved round the short corridor, I came into the room and could tell he was already dead. He was slumped on the one and only piece of furniture - a faded brown, leather sofa with a new stripe of glistening maroon. He had been wearing a puffer jacket and green, combat trousers. He had a shaved head and some uneven stubble. His face was set into the kind of grimace he had probably held since childhood. I examined the body. I found the poor bastard so I was going to have the first look and would inform the authorities in good time. I was careful not to knock anything from where it lay; his box of menthols, stash tin, iPhone. He had been stabbed, which I was sure of because the knife was still sticking out of his chest. I didn't want to go as far as emptying out his pockets. My enthusiasm was swiftly being replaced by nausea and anxiety. Raising myself from where I was stooping, I could feel my blood swell draining heat from my hands and forming splashes of perspiration on my face. I sat down instinctively on the floor and raised my head back against the sofa, not quite touching the corpse. I woke with my head dropped down and I figured I had been out for maybe fifteen minutes. I looked at the arm dangling limply over the side of the sofa. On the wrist I noticed a white plastic wristband with *ST* etched on the side.

Chapter Nineteen

It was a few days until we had the funeral. I did most of the organising and the Jerrys even eased up on us for several days out of apparent respect. The mainland wasn't having the same fortune. I didn't drink at all for a few days, surprising myself, but I smoked too much and drank a lot of coffee. It was actually nice to see some of the Chapman clan again. There was no late night wake, but lots of family get togethers and it reminded me that I didn't have to always pad around the city alone like Sam Spade. The funeral went fine and I had ironed up my uniform all neat the night before. I had sat up late listening to a Duke Ellington, big band record and toasted my mother. The service was respectful and there was a decent turnout. I felt pretty good, actually, once a few days had passed. It was weird. Death and destruction was everywhere, but I felt okay. I didn't feel guilt towards my mother either. In fact, I felt less guilt towards her than I had done in years.

Chapter Twenty

I had cooperated with the emergency services fully and I had no sleep at all that night for my trouble. My benefactor had paid half of my wages with a retainer too if I wanted to track down some more of the gang. He seemed rather pleased with the first outcome, but I did not. I had encountered nicer clients. I searched for more of the gang for a few weeks, but nothing and no one turned up and I lost interest. My triumphant return to the PI game had started on a rather bum note. I spent a few more weeks hanging out in bars, more for leisure I'd admit than for research. I felt uneasy with the case and generally a bit shitty. I saw my doctor a couple of times and he upped my meds. I had my first appointment too with my new social worker.

"Have you had any relapses you wish to tell me about since leaving the hospital Mr. Caskey?" Nicola asked.

"No, I'm doing well thanks," I replied. I had learned my lesson and quit the sarcasm. I didn't have the energy anyhow.

"Good, tell me about how you average day is then," she pressed. She was about forty, slim with expensively peroxided hair and long nails. Her manner was pleasant enough in her slightly countrified, west of Derry accent. But she had an arrogance and condescension that took all of my effort not to try and dismantle a bit.

"Just the usual," I said, "I have my breakfast, watch a bit of TV, have my lunch, sometimes have a walk, you know?" I tried my best to sound mundane, which seemed to work as her face pained in frustration and her forehead wrinkled into thin lines, like a strip of A4. The meeting didn't last long and she didn't seem to make much of an effort to feign interest anyhow.

My flat depressed me as much as anything did. East Belfast is okay and I wasn't even in the worst block of flats, though I was surrounded by some of the most sectarian and backward murals you could imagine. I mostly sat in my small living room, smoking and watching monotonous TV panel shows and repeats of *Friends*. I didn't have enough of the latter to make up a panel team. Feeling sorry for myself and drinking wasn't doing me much good, so I tried to knock both on the head for a time. Staring at my drab living room that was more befitting of a philosophy student was also doing my head in. I took to going for drives all over the city in the evenings listening to mixture of nineties rock and Richard Stark audio books. Living the dream. I felt ill at ease within myself, I couldn't get settled. Then, one night, I was out driving along the Ormeau Road and noticed a group of Christians mingling outside the Ulster Hall. It stands tall and proud; a grand dame of Belfast. There's a big event every month or so there called Manifest that brings out all the teenagers looking for God or girlfriends. It was a long way from some of the uses the hall had provided over the years. In the seventies, it was home of Ian Paisley shouting, "No, no, no" and also where Led Zeppelin first performed "Stairway to Heaven." This group of kids looked about seventeen, were dressed in trendy clothes and singing a praise song of some kind on the steps. There were two guys in dungarees juggling beside them, too. As I slowed, for the car in front to make a right turn, I noticed several of them were wearing white plastic wristbands.

"Have you got a light?"

The group of three stopped their talking over one another and looked at me with disdain.

"No, we don't smoke," the trendiest one said, speaking for the group. He swiped a ginger dreadlock to the side of his face.

"Okay, no bother," I said, "Hey, what's happening in there tonight?"

A girl of about eighteen walked over and I sensed that I was fresh meat. Not my body - my soul.

"It's a revival tonight. Come in if you like, you might find something. We have coffee and cake for everyone too."

She smiled at me and there was a purity in the face looking out at me from a purple hoody, with mahogany hair hanging at the sides.

Now the coffee and cake almost swung it, but I replied, "Thanks, I have to be somewhere. Say, tell me this, I see a lot of you kids are wearing plastic wristbands. What are they for?"

"Oh yeah," she said, and jingled a few ethnic beads out of the way and revealed a band on her own slender arm. If I had been twenty years younger I might have made it my mission to un-convert this one.

"It's for one of the charities we raise money for, Sean's Trust. Haven't you heard of it?"

Of course I already had and I felt like a goat for not thinking of it sooner.

"Yeah, thanks for that," I said, realising I was looking more and more like a letch or a drunk; and there had been times in recent memory when I had been both. "See you around."

"God loves you," she said, after me.

"God loves a try-er," I said, mostly to myself.

***

I walked back to my car and lit up a smoke as I pulled back out into the traffic as some more teenagers filed past with apparent disregard for real world, physical dangers like car wheels. The night I had found the body, the white band had struck me as incongruous on a teenager who might as well have been on a different planet from these guys. My curiosity was well and truly pricked now. *Why would a thieving hood be interested in a local charity like that?* Everyone knew about Sean's Trust. It was setup in memory of Sean Thomas, a local child who had moved with his family to the south of France. I think he had been about thirteen when he was diagnosed with a rare heart condition and he died shortly afterwards. He had been away a few years by then. The story was picked up by the local media and there had been gala balls, fun runs and the like to raise money for the Trust in his name. In many a corner shop or bookies, counters would be adorned by a white plastic collection jar. It seemed the charity had also got into the wristband trend. When I went home I thought about the dead kid with the wristband. I also tried to work out what I should get Billy Chapman to do next. My head was busted. I cleansed my mind with a Bushmills and then listened to some Ledbelly on my turntable. It sounded fucking huge. That's what vinyl is made for. The crackly, old guitar and the gnarly old bastard singing sounded sweet together.

I slept well that night, but woke up with a headache and dog's breath. I took an extra one of my medications, washed down with a fruit juice in the local café. That maybe sounds fairly healthy but it was followed by an "Ulster" and two cups of coffee. I had spent much of the previous night, and even into the morning, googling Sean's Trust. I don't really know why but I was picking at the thread but there is nothing more satisfying than picking at a thread and it coming off between your fingers; or getting a painful skelf out of your fingertip. Unfortunately, it often didn't work out and I wasn't sure yet if it was one of those times. The foundation had been going for about four years and seemingly had been born out of the local community, identifying with a local family who had moved looking for a better life and were instead struck by tragedy. The family, according to the website, had remained very quiet themselves and were still living in France. The charity was being run out of Belfast but I couldn't locate much about the parent company who was organising it. There were countless hits in various, local press and a few YouTube interviews with people connected with the boy's old school and community. There wasn't much information on the family, or the boy himself, apart from the bare details of a family moving away and encountering heartbreak. There was, however, an image of a happy, young boy standing with the cranes of Harland and Wolff in the background. Samson and Goliath stood protectively above this boy with a white football on a terrace, at the end of a quiet street leading to the local football stadium, the Oval. This picture came up again and again in varying edits on collection boxes, t-shirts and posters. I still had an outside notion that something might point me in the direction of the liquor thieves, but I didn't know then that it wouldn't and would, instead, take me somewhere much darker.

Chapter Twenty-One

My office was in chaos. I had treated myself to a little weekend away. Bangor is where anyone, with a few shillings to spend, went during the forties. It is only twelve miles from Belfast; the Amalfi Coast of Northern Ireland. Families went there for sun, sandcastles and a cheap bed and breakfast. I didn't fancy building any sandcastles in May but I managed to sample a few of their pubs. They were okay. One of them even kept the stout barrel under the bar, just the way it should be. I thought about sending Mary a postcard to say that maybe we could meet together again when the war had settled down. Then I caught myself on for being a goat because I had only met the woman once. Anyway, the break seemed to do me some good. Nothing had happened to my office over the weekend. It's just I usually clean it on a Friday and when I say clean it I mean sweep all of my old newspapers and cigarette ends into a bin. It was eleven on Monday morning and I felt terrible. I'm not an anxious kind of person, but my routine was all mixed up and my head was washed out with liquor. It had been a couple of weeks since the funeral and I hadn't been in my office since before the Causeway. Then my phone rang.

***

"Yeah? Uh huh. No, I'm him. Yeah. Well, alright. That's fine. I'll be there."

It was the housekeeper for a family called Morris. Their address was on The Malone Road and they had a housekeeper, so they must be doing okay for themselves. The lady of the house, Edith, wanted to see me at twelve-thirty at her place. It sounded like they could afford to pay well and I was more than happy to clean my office another time.

I had a little lunch at home in East Belfast; some broth and a Belfast bap roll. A cup of tea armed my blood a little more. It was dry outside, so I reluctantly got on my bicycle. I had overspent in Bangor and it was the cheapest form of transport though not the safest. I almost came off twice. The city centre was still in recovery after the most recent bombing spree. That had been the nice thing about Bangor, only twelve miles away but the war might never have even been on. Just like Antrim without the Giants.

I arrived close enough to the arrival time and wheeled my bicycle up the small incline to the house. I'm no architect but this was a pretty fancy place. Not a mansion but very agreeable from where I was standing.

"This way please, Sir," the butler said, leading me inside before I could ring the bell. We strode through a hallway, guarded by stag heads and a lonely, stuffed, grizzly bear.

"Please wait here," he said, crisply and left before I could get any words out. I looked around and drank in a stunning sitting room ,Duck-egg walls, leather sofas and imposing portraits all lit by a marble open fire. I padded around a little then went to light a cigarette. No lighter. I must have dropped it on the jerky cycle over. I looked about for a light. No luck. I hovered my cigarette over the open fire. The door opened as the flames licked at my fingers.

"Damn," I growled, instinctively and sucked my fingers. The distinguished woman who entered did not react, but simply closed the door and walked a few paces into the room. She was taller than most women and she only enhanced the elegance of the room.

"Are you quite alright?" she asked, pleasantly.

"Yeah. I'm sorry, I burnt my fingers. Is it okay if I smoke?"

"Certainly, please," she gestured to the two seats by the fire. We sat down. She looked to me to be around fifty years old with kind eyes and disposition.

"What can I do for you, Mrs. Morris?" I asked.

"Mr. Chapman, I understand you are good at what you do, private detection. I have a job for you that requires the utmost discretion."

I looked more closely at her. Her eyes had a little sadness to them too.

"I can guarantee that, Mrs. Morris."

"I have a very serious matter that I need help with. I cannot go to the police...."

She actually looked a little broken.

"It's alright, take your time," I said.

"My daughter did not come home on Friday night instead I received this letter through the door. Please."

She handed me across the letter and her face pained as I read it out loud.

"Dear Mrs. Morris, we have your daughter. She is safe. If you inform the police of this letter, she will not be. The ransom is £5,000. We will contact you again soon."

I put the letter on the table and sat back a little, rubbing at my chin.

"I'm very sorry Mrs. Morris," I said, truthfully.

"Thank you. Will you take the case?" she asked, anxiously.

"What does your husband think about this?"

"He was killed last year at sea, Royal Navy." Her face grew darker still.

"I'm sorry. I was in the 38ᵗʰ Irish myself," I offered. *"What is it you would like me to do, exactly, Mrs. Morris?"*

She stood up and walked over to an impressive Waterford glass drinks cabinet.

"What would you like to drink?" she asked, instead.

"I'll take a whiskey, please."

She mixed herself a gin and tonic and handed me a Scotch. I would have preferred Irish, but it was hardly the time to say. My mind's eye flitted briefly to Bushmills and The Causeway.

"I want you to dig for me Mr. Chapman. I think you would have a better chance than me and, to be frank, I barely have the energy to deal with this at all. It is only myself and Laura here now. That's my daughter."

She briefly gazed out at the intricate fountain that was gently bubbling in the formal gardens.

"Have you any idea who could have done this, Mrs. Morris?"

"I truly do not. I have thought through all possibilities. My husband had a few enemies, of course, the same as any man. You may presume us very wealthy Mr. Chapman, but I do not have an endless pot of money. We have only kept on two servants now who stay more out of loyalty than for any fiscal gain. Since my husband passed away the family businesses have suffered too. I am not claiming to be a pauper, but to raise five thousand pounds would be a great struggle; I possibly would have to sell my home. I want your help mostly because I am not certain that, even if I raised the money, I would get my daughter back safely."

She stood suddenly and turned her back to fix us both another drink. She dabbed at her eyes.

"I will do whatever I can, Mrs. Morris. I can start right away. Tell me about your daughter, please."

She told me about Laura Morris, who was a girl of twenty one, studying History in her third year at Queen's University, Belfast. Less than a quarter of students were female at the time and they needed to outshine the men. Laura sounded like a self-sufficient type, someone who did not want to rely on her privileged upbringing. Apparently, she was a good daughter to her mother and was never in any trouble. Mrs. Morris did not want for me to say to anyone that she was missing, but suggested I begin by speaking with her best friend and also a young man she was seemingly courting.

***

I started with the boyfriend. It did not take me long to find out where Jack Riley usually spent his afternoons. The third bar I tried was The Crown. The barman told me which patron he was before pouring me a pint of stout. The Crown had once been a favourite haunt of mine in my younger days, too. Jack looked to be a dandy, floppy hair and a twice too big scarf engulfing his neck. If this had been on the mainland he would have struggled to avoid the draft and I don't think he would have lasted long one way or another. He sat with two girls who were apparently hanging on his every word.

"Hello Jack. I am Dr Chapman, I have your test results. Ladies, will you please excuse us?"

Jack stared blankly at me and the girls split. I sat down opposite him in a corner booth.

"What is this all about? I am not waiting on test results and you look little like a doctor." He flounced his ridiculous hair as he spoke.

"That may be true, but I look a lot like a detective, now pipe down. I'm a friend of Mrs. Morris, Laura's mother. It seems Laura went away suddenly. What do you know about it?"

I studied him. I knew how to deal with a little peacock like that one.

"Nothing. I mean what is this? Laura? I haven't seen the girl in ages. She's really quite tiresome. What do you want from me?"

"When did you last see her?" I asked, coolly.

"Well, of course, I saw her at lectures last week but we haven't spent any time together really if that's what you mean. I saw her at the Great War lecture on Friday afternoon, it would have been." He looked like the puff in

him had been squeezed a little. "We had a thing going, maybe for a while, but I've moved on, alright?"

"If you're holding out on me I'll come back and find you."

He sat up straight and patted his scarf down flat around his shoulder. "I am not lying to you. Come back if you want to."

"Okay, well if you think of anything, give me a call." I handed him my card and left the rest of my drink. I wasn't thirsty anymore.

Chapter Twenty-Two

I was down the Belmont Road by ten the next morning, not with a spring in my step, but certainly a minor twinge. I had a few messages to run that I had been putting off, but started with a tasty fry up in Oliver's. The message I really had to make, but had been particularly avoiding, was to the bank.

"Mr. Monaghan will see you now."

I was shown into the little side office of Strandtown Bank by the ever monotone secretary, without so much of an offer of caffeine. Jim Monaghan was finishing a phone call, and his own caffeinated drink from his thermos cup. I took a seat at the desk that rather crowded the small, Ikea-styled room.

"Brian, I'm glad you came in," he said, with an audible sigh. Jim was my age, we had schooled and truanted together and he had set into pre middle age with easy abandon. He wasn't a bad sort, but he was very arrogant. He had a grumpy side too, he claimed, only when his blood sugars were low, but I think the credit crunch contributed more to it.

"I meant to come in sooner, but you know how things are. I wasn't too well there actually...."

"Sorry to hear that," he cut in." You have been a hard man to track down, though, certainly. We need to get your repayments sorted out."

"I know, I know, I actually have had a good bit of work and I intend on paying off those figures as my next priority."

"Brian, I really need a little more than that," he said, picking up a few loose pages and fixing them with a paperclip.

"Sure, I understand, I'll come back in a few days and give you the definites, okay?"

I stood and took a step towards the door.

"Brian," he said, urgently. "It is getting quite serious. I would be remiss not to say so. I know there used to be two of you paying the mortgage and you're left to...."

"I'll pay you," I said firmly, opening the door. "I just need a few days. See you, Jim."

***

"Fucking Caskey, ya wee prick."

"How are you Jemma?"

We sat down in the second studio of Belfast Giant FM (They liked to say the FM stood for Finn McCool).

She handed me a coffee that made me feel even more welcome than her opening banter.

"I'm the best Bri, fabulous. How 'bout you, you went off the radar there for a bit, did you?"

It was hard to tell if she was being tactful or just making small talk. She pulled her purple hair back off her face and clipped it into a bun. She was looking good. Jemma was pushing forty and we had knocked about together over the years, professionally and otherwise. Not romantically though, so to speak. She was a good girl, a journalist by trade she had worked all over the place and had been doing a spell with the news team at the radio station.

"I suppose I've been keeping a bit of a low profile alright, that's true. I've been working on 'The Great Northern Irish Novel,' seems no one has got around to it yet."

"Some have had a go," she smiled, taking a sip of her black coffee with those full bodied lips of hers. "So, is this a social call?"

"Yes, will you marry me?"

"Okay... but I want an open relationship."

"I couldn't live with that Jemma, I take it back. Okay, you got me, I'm after a bit of a favour."

"Those mics aren't on are they?" I asked, gesturing to the various recording equipment in the little studio.

"They are, I like having all my proposals on tape. So, a favour?"

"Yes, please."

"I knew it you shit. You're such a user! Go on then, what can I do you for?"

"Do you remember the nineteen year old that got stabbed up in North Belfast? Name of Mat Rooney."

"Em, yeah, yeah I do. I did the usual follow up on it, but the police didn't kill themselves over it from what I could tell. It was just put down to the usual gang kinda thing. What's your interest?"

I told her about how I got involved in the case, but not about my Sean's Trust angle. I didn't want her to think I was completely crazy.

"I was hoping to speak with one of his mates. Maybe get a bit of info to what he was involved in, kind of off the record thing. I think there might be a wider scope to it, if there is, I'll gladly send the story your way."

"Sure, I could probably get you a name, call in a favour if I need to. It'll cost you though." She crossed her legs and pouted.

"I'll buy you dinner. The Park Avenue and down to the Oval for a match."

"Oh, you sure now how to treat a girl. I'll take the dinner, but I'd rather paint the Oval and watch it dry as soon as watch Irish League."

"You cut me deep, Jem."

**

"Please take a seat Mr. Caskey."

The school secretary of Avoniel High in East Belfast gestured to a row of three red, plastic seats in a hall by the principal's office.

"Thank you and thanks for the coffee."

She smiled briefly and returned to her own office. I sat alone in a hall lined with photographs of headmasters, First Elevens and local minor celebrities. I hunched over on the plastic chair and considered my shoes could do with a clean.

"Sorry to keep you," a voice said, from the door that had shot open, temporarily hiding the speaker. I stood up and stepped towards the door. A tall and sturdy, but not fat man offered me his hand.

"Hi, Brian Caskey," I said, and shook his hand, looking into his warm, but deep set eyes.

"I'm James Cleary, the principle of our little academy, come in."

We sat and drank a coffee, talking some pleasantries about the weather, school league tables, local football, the seventies and lastly Sean Thomas. I received the same blurb I had already got time over from Google. Then I got a lot about how the school had done a genuinely, impressive amount of fundraising, in a community in need of some regeneration and community togetherness.

"Tell me a bit more about Sean," I said, finally, after boring of the school marketing ad.

"Well, yes of course," he said, crossing his legs a little awkwardly. He looked uncomfortable in his tight black suit and blue shirt. "Unfortunately, I did not know the boy personally," he offered, almost apologetically.

I kept a steady look and didn't offer any further communication, verbal or otherwise.

"You see, he was only really here a few months before moving away," he continued eventually. "He was in first year, and those first few months everyone is just settling in, and we had a large change in staff around that time too."

He went on to give me some more snapshots of a person and nothing more than that solitary photograph had already suggested; a pleasant and kind young man from a working class background, good to his family, enjoyed playing football and supported The Glens.

"Could I speak to someone who knew him better than yourself then, please, Mr. Cleary?"

He sighed just short of audible and replied quietly, "As I said, we had several changes in staff and Sean sadly wasn't at the school for very long at all."

The atmosphere had shifted slightly and I felt increasingly in control, despite being well past my next due medication.

"Could you show me the records of those attending from that year?"

"Mr. Caskey, that would be most unusual when you really have no remit here," he replied, more flustered.

"I think you should prefer talking to me and not the police," I suggested, firmly.

"Well," he said, heaving for a breath. "I really think this meeting may be over. I have absolutely nothing to hide unequivocally. I do not appreciate this questioning and...."

"I don't think you even know if he definitely went to your school," I interrupted. "And, I think it would be quite the embarrassment if it came out that the school didn't know if a pupil had even attended or hadn't."

I was surprised by his sudden regression to silence as he rested back into his chair.

I pressed further. "Just so you know, this is part of an investigation that I'm looking into involving a murder. The police are investigating that murder as well and at the moment they are not connecting it to this school as I have done."

"Okay, look, I am speaking to you openly and I would like our conversation to remain between us. I'm trying to cooperate with you. Okay? I certainly know nothing about any murder or anything like that," he added, breathily.

"You don't want me talking to the police then?"

"No, I mean, damn it Caskey. I'd like you to be delicate if you can."

"Okay, I'm not out to get you I'll keep whatever I can quiet if I'm able to," I offered.

"Alright well," he said, leaning forward and pressing both his hands onto the desk. "You could say we don't have any official record of his attendance. I mean nothing that I can solidly hold up to scrutiny if you like. There's no reason to think he didn't go here but our computer system was undergoing maintenance and most information was kept on paper, but we know the records aren't perfect."

"So no one even remembers him at all?" I said, trying not to sound so taken aback as I was that my hunch had been right.

"Well, no, I suppose not but there really isn't any reason to think that it's all a lie. I mean why would anyone say that? We didn't realise there may be this issue until sometime into the media frenzy and after we had spoken several times to the press ourselves. It was too late to... well look deeper into it."

"And it suited you to have some good PR for the school up till then. You've done well out of it since then too. Have you even met his parents?"

"I've had lots of contact with them, a lovely family. Though, no, I haven't actually met them but we have been in regular email contact for several years now. I am sure the boy went here, but am ashamed to say we do not have the records that we should have, that is all."

He was almost pleading now. I couldn't believe my luck.

"Thank you, Mr. Cleary, you've been most helpful."

***

I stopped for a bite, a pint and a few smokes at The Great Eastern and then spent the afternoon trawling door to door all around Dee street and out towards Sydenham. I had a fondness for these old, tired terraces. I had kicked about them as a kid though never kicked as far as The Oval. I caught a lot of people who were in and were up for a chat. Mostly, these were young mothers with children wrapped around their necks and retired men watching repetitive TV about bargain hunting and home improvements. I got a lot of blurbs and sound bites, the same as what I already knew. I also had a lot of people who thought such and such knew the family better and a friend of a friend was a family friend. I didn't speak to one person who knew the boy, or the family, directly. It was a long, few hours but it didn't leave me dejected and it made me think that this just backed up the theories I was starting to form.

"A pint of Bass shandy please," I asked, after leaving the daylight for the dinge and grime of The Belmont Arms. It made the Eastern look like a Soho members club. The gruff barman gave me a disapproving look and searched to see if he could find any lemonade. I didn't feel the need to explain I was trying to keep a clear head.

"Is there a lady joining you?" he asked, winking at me.

"Fuck off, where's Mo?" I asked, in a friendly tone and informing him that I was a local.

"Off today. Too many vodkas and coke."

"Okay."

"Enjoy your cocktail," he said, setting the drink up on an already sodden bar mat.

I had a sip and glanced about me. It was a small, working man's bar and one that I had gone to many times over the years for information. Particularly, when I was in the force and had enough knowledge to put the squeeze on people, I often found it liable to bear fruit out of its mud and decay. It hadn't changed much since I was last in. Two, small TV's were mounted at each end of the room; the bar stretching the length in front of the tables. The wooden floor was stained with all sorts and nobody cared, the green upholstery was ripped and faded and nobody cared, the women's toilet was out of order, but nobody needed it. Of the five or six in the bar, I recognised half. When I clocked a man's peroxide head bobbing around as he plunged coins into the poker machine in the side alcove, I knew who best to talk to. I headed straight over to him, the flickering lights becoming more garish and the tinny tune from the machine more irritating. Eric had a pint of cider in one hand and was doing a nervous shuffle as he continued playing the game with the other.

"It's not gonna pay out, you're playing it wrong," I said, moving closer.

Eric turned round with a start and then broke into a broad smile.

"Brian, ya big fruit, what about you?"

He gave me a slap on the back and took a swig of his pint, considering me. Eric was the most effeminate person I've met but, for some reason, insists on calling everyone a "fruit" all the time. He was five-foot-ten, stocky and had the gift of the gab. He had been a good informer for me over the years and somehow managed to never fall foul of the big guns. He was as camp as Rocky Horror at Christmas, but he had an edge and could handle himself.

"Will we have a seat Eric? I'd like a wee chat."

"Sure mate, a catch up, aye, good. Now just gimme a wee second, you go over there sure."

I snagged a table and checked for any bodily fluids on the chair before sitting down. I looked on for a few minutes as Eric sank another sixty or seventy quid into the machine.

"Fuck, fuck, fuck!" he shouted, at the machine in half jest and came over to sit with me.

"Been a long time Brian," he said, stretching out a bit.

"Has indeed, this shithole is just the same though."

"Aye, it is alright."

"Things okay yourself?"

"Yeah, can't complain. Look," he said, swiveling his leg further into the booth. "I'm sorry to hear things have been rough for you... terrible thing that accident."

My heart instantly started to race and I thought to myself that was a funny way to put it - *There was no fucking accident*, but I kept under control and pushed my feelings back down again where they should be.

"Thanks Eric, I'm alright. Look, you could be a help to me maybe."

I told him about the murder and the wristband and the school. He seemed to listen carefully until an older man started to play the machine and Eric became distracted.

Crash! Plop, plop, plop went the machine as it emptied out dozens of pound coins.

"Cunt," Eric said, under his breath. "Sorry, Brian, carry on."

We chatted for a bit and agreed on what I would pay him, depending on the kind of information he turned up. How many "drink tokens" he would get as he liked to call it. We went out for a smoke together and parted after agreeing to talk again in a day or two. I felt I was getting somewhere, or was at least trying. Nothing made me more certain that I was on the right track than what happened at about six o'clock. The sunlight had gone and it was setting in to be a cold and wet autumn evening. It hadn't started to rain yet and I decided to walk back to my car just a street from where I had finished my calls earlier.

"Hey Brian," came a voice. I turned towards the calm, thick voice and was struck in the face giving me a large, thick lip. There were two of them. The second drove a fist into my stomach knocking my pie and chips out onto the curb. I doubled over. One of them lay a boot into my face for good measure.

"Back off, Caskey," the same voice said, firmly. Then they strode away, not running. I didn't back off. I didn't do anything but lie right where I was. Minutes went by and a few drops of rain fell on my bruised and slightly, bloodied face. I sat up a little. I then tried to stand and a wave passed over me. I woke up drenched from the rain and the wave. I ached. Somehow, I got to my car and then to home. Whiskey, a bath and cigarettes helped me get to sleep and I didn't wake again properly for nearly fourteen hours.

...thump...

"There's some sort of noise,"

"You might need to wake up a bit."

"No."

...thump...

"What is that?"

"It's inside your head."

"Oh."

Dawn light... coldness beyond the covers... pain.

"Need to sleep."

I didn't venture out till early the next afternoon. I needed to get my weekly prescription, cigarettes and some first aid supplies. Unfortunately, the chemist had recently stopped selling cigs, so I had to make two stops. I went home and there were two answering machine messages waiting for me; one from the bank and one from my social worker. All I'd need was one from the Voluntary Sector. I kind of shut down in one way for the rest of the day: but not completely because I wrote and wrote and wrote.

Chapter Twenty-Three

My next stop was at Laura's friend's house, down a short way off the Lisburn road. It was modest compared to the Morris home. Still, it was three times the size of where I lived. It was almost five in the evening and she was home. She lived with her aunt who was away at the time. The whole downstairs was being re-wired for electricity, so she took me up to her bedroom.

"Can I call you Billy?" she asked. She closed the door and sat on the bed. I took off my hat and sat on the solitary chair. It was really a traditional kid's bedroom, now inhabited by a rather messy, young undergraduate.

"You can call me whatever you would like Ms Ward." I crossed my legs.

"Lizzy, please."

"Okay."

She looked about twenty three, long brown hair and green eyes. Ten years my junior but, I have to say, she was quite a knock out.

"Cigarette?" she offered.

"Yes, thanks." I lit hers first. I had bought a box of matches at the Crown. It was a safer way to light up for my fingers.

"So, a gumshoe in my room?" she giggled, impishly. "Whatever could you want with me?" She kicked off her shoes and propped her back up against the wall. She was as innocent as a wheel is square. I had to compose myself a little.

"Ms Ward... Lizzy, your friend Laura...."

"Is she alright?" she asked, keenly.

"She's gone away quite suddenly and her Mother wants me to ask around, check that she's okay. It should be nothing to worry about."

"Oh," she said, rolling her cigarette around her dark red lips. "Okay. I last saw her Thursday, I think. Yes, Thursday. We don't go to the same lessons. I'm studying music, but we had lunch then and she seemed fine."

"Anything unusual about her? Anything at all?"

"I don't think so. Wait, well, she did seem quite excitable. Yes, she didn't say much, but she seemed very pleased about something."

"Do you have any idea what it could have been about?"

"I don't, I've no idea," her face brightened. "That must be it though, I suppose that's why she's taken off. I wouldn't worry about Laura. She's very independent. She's always got something new going on."

I stood. "Thank you very much for your time," I said.

"Going so soon? Can I not fetch you a drink or something?" she pouted.

"No, no, you're very kind." I fumbled for the door. "If you think of anything else, please give me a call."

I pressed my card down on her makeup desk and briskly went down the stairs and out the door before she could stand up. The cold air felt good on my face.

The next morning I woke up to my home phone ringing. Sometimes I wished I hadn't put both numbers on my card.

"Hello?" I croaked.

"I'm sorry to wake you, this is Edith."

It took a second to register.

"Hello, Mrs. Morris." I propped myself up on one arm and pulled the sheet back. It felt cold in the room and I pulled it back again.

"I have received another letter," she said, soberly. "They say I have a month to get the money together. They will arrange where I have to drop it. Mr. Chapman, they said again if I inform the police that they will... harm her. What should I do?"

"Mrs. Morris, sit tight if you can for a few days. Let me see how far I can get and then we can think about the police. Okay?"

"Alright, Mr. Chapman, I trust you."

She hung up. I think she would have sounded somber no matter what I had to say. I wondered if she was thinking the same as me - that her daughter was probably already dead.

***

I couldn't sleep after that. I had some tea and toast and put my other grey suit on. I was out of the house by nine in the morning. I don't think I had seen nine outside before that. It was a nice day, so I decided to walk to Queen's University. It took around fifty minutes. Her mother informed me, at our first meeting, that Laura had two lecturers, so I thought I'd go and speak with them both. The main part of the university is a pretty, impressive building. It is one of many buildings in Belfast built by the architect Lanyon. I do know a little of my Gaudi from my gaudy. I had a smoke on the grounds and then strolled over to University Square. The row of innocuous, Georgian houses beside the main University were, in fact, all lecture halls and offices. Behind the façade they were fully renovated and linked by a rear corridor. The tree lined street looked striking in the frosty sun. It was good weather and it reminded me of my last day at the Causeway and my rather inglorious exit.

"Do you know where the English office is?" a pretty young student asked me, outside the row of houses.

"I'm sorry, I don't. I'm looking for the History Department myself," I said.

"Thanks anyway, I think history is down the end mister." She bustled off with her friends in a giggle.

I found the house and was fortunate that Mr. Martineau was keeping office hours until lunch. He specialised in The Great War and Military History. His secretary got me a cup of tea and a chair. I was soon told to go on up to his office - Room 105. I knocked lightly on the oak panelled door.

"Enter, please."

A thick, French accent called me in and I opened the door, surveying the room.

"Monsieur Chapman, please have a seat." He gestured to a sofa by his desk as he sat back down on his finely, upholstered chair.

It was a good sized office blanketed in books. There hung an aroma of pipe tobacco in the air complimenting the mustiness of the aging books.

"I am told by my secretary that I may be of some assistance to you?" He leaned lightly on the desk.

"Yes, Mr. Martineau, I appreciate you seeing me at short notice." I took off my hat.

"My pleasure detective; can I offer you anything perhaps?" He gestured flamboyantly to a sideboard laden with auburn drinks and cigars. He looked to be in his early fifties and was almost six foot. He wore a pinstriped suit and brown toupee and he wore them both well.

"No, thanks. Can you tell me what you know about Laura Morris?"

"Ah, oui, she is a bright student of mine. Alas, I know her only a little. She is not in any trouble I hope?" He took out his pipe and began preparing it.

"No, nothing like that, her mother just wants to see how she is getting on."

"Good, good," he purred, as he struck a match. *"A fine student, above average indeed. She is one of my best*

since I arrived here a few months ago. I am afraid that I can be of little help to you."

"Has she been attending all of her classes recently? Have you noticed any change in her at all?" I pressed.

"No, Mr. Chapman, I could not say I have noticed anything. And, yes, I believe she has attended all of my lectures," he replied, evenly.

I stood up.

"Well, thanks again for your time."

I replaced my hat. He rose and offered me his hand.

"Au revoir, Mr. Chapman."

***

It was not time for lunch yet but my stomach was beginning to remind me I had been up early and it would not wait long. I decided to call on Laura's other lecturer while I was there. When I got to the lecture hall, it was five to midday. I waited outside the door smoking as an array of students filed past me looking pretty eager to escape the lecture room. I went in.

"Mr. McCord?" I asked, approaching the lectern dusted in sheets on Irish History 1603-1641 and the plump man beside it hastily gathering them up.

"Yes?" he answered, absently, not looking up. He spoke with a gentrified, Dublin brogue.

"The name's Billy Chapman, I'm a Private Detec...."

"Private Detective?" he interrupted, looking up.

"Yes, nothing to worry about, I'm just looking for some background information."

He looked well into middle age with a ruddy face, no neck and a rotund lower half reminding me a little of Loach.

"Oh?" he said, returning back to his tidying. "I'm rather busy but how can I help?"

"What can you tell me about Laura Morris?"

"Err," he seemed to have misplaced something. "Laura, yes, she's a good student. Oh, she isn't any bother is she?" He looked up again, pausing for a moment.

"No, I don't think so, is there any reason she might be?"

"I really wouldn't know. I only see her a few hours a week."

"Can you think of any trouble she may have got into? It's just her mother is worried about her."

"Well, I don't really know, but she is quite the headstrong girl. Likes to challenge authority. You know the sort."

He seemed happy he had found everything and began to walk towards the exit.

"Sorry, I couldn't be more help to you Chapman," he said.

I walked along with him, I had little choice.

"Is there anyone else with whom I could speak to about Laura, do you think, Mr. McCord?"

He pondered, less distracted.

"I suppose you've talked to some of her friends. Have you gone to see the Frenchie?"

"Yes, yes I have."

"The only other place would be The Belfast Telegraph."

"Go on?" I said.

"Yes, I believe she helps out there quite a bit, researching stories and the like. I'd have no idea who she works with, but it could be worth a call."

"Thank you, I will."

I left him to flurry on his way.

***

It was certainly an acceptable lunch time now and I enjoyed a mostly, liquid lunch in White's Tavern. It is one of many, local pubs professing to be the oldest in all of Ireland; some claim for an island associated with alcoholism. Whether it was or it wasn't, it did offer a quiet and pleasant spot to sit in for a while. I had a lot to think about. Something felt fishy about the whole ransom setup, but I wasn't sure what yet. I had now spoken to five people close to Laura and nothing seemed to be much of a lead, no break in the case as yet. I just felt like I was rearranging deck chairs on Titanic. There was a chance she was still alive. I hoped my next stop would shine even a small chink of light. My mind wandered strangely back to the Causeway and I thought about the case there for a moment. It still didn't sit quite right with me. There was something wrong and it annoyed me that I didn't know what. It was probably nothing much, I said, to myself and dragged my legs up and walked on to the telegraph offices. I'd say I felt I'd left a part of me up at the Causeway but that'd be sentimental.

***

It was a hive of activity, important looking people looked self-important. Even the paperboys might have been running a multi-national. I waited, patiently, as various secretaries asked me, "Can I help you?" after their predecessors had apparently got distracted by something else and not come back. After some first class, investigative journalism, they worked out who I should speak to. Eventually, I was brought in to see A.P Turner, a well-known, local journalist. I was familiar with his work. He had traveled widely as a war correspondent and was something of a local personality.

"Nice to meet you, Mr. Turner," I said, and meant it.

"Mr. Chapman, please take a seat."

I sat across the desk from the well-groomed, charismatic man in his early forties. The office was a haven from the rest of the building. Everything in there seemed organised and calm.

"Can I get you a coffee sent up?" He gestured slightly to the phone.

"No, thank you though."

I explained, again, my patter of how I was doing a little research for Laura's mother and if he could be of any assistance. He agreed with the consensus that Laura was both a bright and enthusiastic, young girl.

"Laura has assisted me with many of my articles, Mr. Chapman and she is, quite frankly, leagues ahead of most who have been in employ here for years. If she is still set on a career in journalism after her degree, I will do everything possible to secure her a job with us," he said, ardently.

"Was there anything in particular that she was working on at present, Mr. Turner?"

"Well, yes, there has been one project she has been researching. I trust I can rely on your discretion. I wouldn't want our competitors to publish a similar story before us you understand."

"Of course, mum's the word, please go on."

"For a while now we have been preparing something of an expose'."

He looked me in the eye and took a breath.

"Mr. Chapman, the war is only young. Before it, we were only separate from the South with a political divide. Now there is an international boundary clearly there and a very different foreign policy. There are many Krauts living south of the border for example. The same could certainly not be said of up here. My suspicion is that some may be working for the Nazi regime." He swung a little on his chair.

"Well, yes, I would be sure there would be Germans but not Nazis, necessarily. I'm ex-services but I still know the difference. I suppose there would be some spies about like in France and some colony hot spots."

"Yes, that is true," he said, excitedly clasping his hands. "But, they also have turned up in every part of the world. If you were to look throughout the press of many foreign countries, as I have, you would see how prominent it is. I believe some have made it here into our small country too, Mr. Chapman." He sat back.

"Really?" I was quite bemused. "Is there much evidence?"

"Ha, ha! Of course, you are a detective! Yes, there is and it is not all so fantastic. There have been several proven cases of Nazis living in Eire. The high profile cases had them leave as De Valera and the Irish government would not want to appear less than neutral. In saying that it was decent of them, truthfully, for sending so many fire regiments during the bad raid up to us here. At present, no, there is nothing to suggest that any have come up here. But that is what I intend to find out."

I must have had a strange expression as he seemed to enjoy gazing at it.

We chatted for some time. I was fascinated by what he had to say and he seemed to enjoy the conversation too. He, apparently, was in no big rush to get back to his work.

"Laura has been invaluable to me in snooping around, following up on sources and even looking into specific suspect's records. A lovely girl and I truly hope that she is alright."

"Well, I appreciate the time you have given me. Please, may I ask one more thing from you, Mr. Turner?"

"Certainly," he said, gesturing with both hands.

"Is there any way I can see what Laura was last working on exactly? Does she have a desk or something?"

"Well, let me see. No, she doesn't have a desk but she does have a locker where she keeps all of her current documents and notes. Laura, to be honest, was the first to start me on the road to this particular piece of journalism,

Mr. Chapman, and I sincerely hope that there is nothing the matter with her."

"It's just for her mother's benefit you understand. I want to rule out this part of her life with her absence. Can I have access to these documents? I will sign for them and return them tomorrow, or I could arrange a written request from Mrs. Morris...."

"That won't be necessary, I will arrange it all for you immediately." He stood.

"I appreciate it," I said. I didn't enjoy lying to him about the situation. He was the first person I had met, other than her mother, who seemed to genuinely care about Laura.

*** *

I took the bus back to my flat, took off my tie, hat and jacket and stretched out. I was pooped. I made some dinner, had a Bushmills and tried to relax with a bit of music. Ledbelly sang on my record player about the TB blues. I didn't have TB but I still kind of knew how he felt. I had a friend who had kept me up to date on the best new releases before the war. There weren't many new releases coming through anymore in those days and anyway he was dead. Killed in the early blitz, he went to the wrong air raid shelter; just crummy luck. I thought about my mother and her own bad luck. It felt strange, still, that I accepted her death so easily. I don't know. I knew she was at peace and I felt at peace with that I suppose. I had decided I needed an hour or two before I could trawl through Laura's papers. But much sooner than that I'd thought, I couldn't wait any longer, I lit up a Lucky and dove in. There was a lot to read; clippings, copies of official documents and her notebook. Much of it I could see how it linked in as research for Turner's theory. Some of it was pretty silly. There were various articles from local newspapers concerning local butchers, bus conductors and haberdashers who could allegedly have been the next

Goring. There were maps and diagrams drawn into the little notebook, too. There seemed to be a lot of meandering theories being worked on. In over half of the pages, I did not see an obvious link to Nazi escape routes at all. I tried to not get too carried away myself. I needed to remember that, in the first place, I was looking for a person and not a Maltese Falcon. But, then, I found some pages all about some place outside of Dublin. It was called Kantian Park. I had no idea what it was. What did interest me was all the asterisks Laura had put on them and bits underlined. Then she had written in pencil beside it: 15.30 Belfast Central.

***

I had called on Mrs. Morris in the early evening and she had kindly given me some cake and tea. She also gave me enough cash to pay for my train ticket to Dublin and a nice hotel. I explained to her that I only had a hunch but she agreed that if I was up for the task then it was worth checking it out. She seemed a little brighter to see we at least had a lead. That night, I packed and felt good that this case was going somewhere. I hadn't been to Dublin for years and I'd look forward to seeing it again. I hoped I wouldn't resent every man between eighteen and fifty that I saw. I had no idea what kind of a place I was looking to find there, exactly and what I might uncover, but I had an address and that was a start. I took off my army stripes and placed them in the drawer with my uniform. I tended to wear them as much for pride as to avoid being attacked for being a conchie. Down South I'd rather not be attacked for being a Brit.

Chapter Twenty-Four

Losing myself in the writing had done me some good. My mind was refocused, ready to look from a different angle at what was in front of me. Sometimes, I'd love to be able to look at myself that way. I was always too scared to try mushrooms, but always imagined that's what it would be like. I had enough vices already to keep the squad in business, so I'd stick with the writing for a time longer. I felt fresh though I hadn't had the best night's sleep. I had dreamt some kind of stressful dream, but couldn't recall the detail. All I could remember was someone was suddenly there, who shouldn't be, and that I was shit scared. That's when I woke up and shouted out. I had these kind of dreams all the time and I think I must have conditioned myself to do that to wake myself up out of them. My wife used to tease me about not being not much of a macho cop. That next afternoon I spent with new best friend, Google. I looked at the photograph again and again and it certainly was possible that a random boy had been photo-shopped in. It had an uncomfortable atmosphere about it, but I couldn't think how. I found myself gazing at the stripes on the football, the shadow on the cranes for minutes at a time, but no epiphany. *Were there any tell-tell signs? The question would then be why would someone do that with it anyway? What possible purpose?* I spent about an hour searching the internet for "young boy with a football." There were millions of hits. Probably billions. I possibly would have got fewer hits if just searching for the word "porn." Again, the lack of clarity didn't depress me. It just made me realise that it was something else in my theory that was potentially possible. I was stretching, I was experimenting. It felt good and it had been a long time. I then spent the evening delving into anything I could find about the parent company of the Trust. It took much delving and a good deal of drinking. I stopped for a while in the early evening and ordered in a Chinese. Now, this carryout round the corner from me lets you do half portions of dishes and half chip, half rice for free. Fuckin' sweet! Well, it was sweet, and sour and also curried. I paused from the drink for a while and had a cup of coffee before getting back to it. What I found was a definite link to one company and it appeared that they may well have gone to a great deal of trouble to disguise this fact. It looked all legal, but purposefully concealed. I suppose a bit like the difference between those politicians that tax evade and those who tax avoid. Screaming Tree was a media firm based out of Civic Street in Belfast centre. Their main business appeared to be in PR and Marketing. I was encouraged to discover they also had a small holding in the south of France.

During my post dinner nap, Jemma rang me and gave me a name. It was a friend of the deceased who was willing to talk if kept secret and for a bit of cash.

"Hi, I'm looking for Greg."

"Oh yeah, come in."

A stereotype of a student with long ginger hair, who would fail every drugs test possible, showed me in. It was an old, Victorian house off the Lisburn road, usual five bed student digs.

"Go on in there," he said, pointing to a snug den at the back of the house.

I went in and took a seat in an old, brown arm chair leaving the leather, two seater beside it.

"Hi, I'm Greg," the man said, warmly as he entered and shut the door. He looked about in his early twenties, but confident and comfortable in his large frame. He had a side parting in his black hair and would have had a look of Boris Johnson if he'd been blonde.

"So Greg," I started, easing back into the chair. "I believe you have some information for me."

"Yes, I do," he said, casually, sitting down onto the sofa. "You have the money?"

I took out the folded bills and set them on the mantle of the old fireplace.

"There it is. If you tell me something useful it's yours."

"Good then," he said, brightly. "If you want, I could try and find out more information if that was something you'd like."

"Yes, it could be, but let's hear what you know now."

"Okay," he said, inching forward, his hands clasped together as if in confession. "First off, we agree this is just between us?"

"Of course."

"Okay. I also want you to know that I didn't have anything to do with Mat's... enterprises. We had been friends since primary school and still kept in touch... I think he liked having someone who wasn't involved in that other part of his life."

He looked at me for some kind of reaction.

"Go on," I said.

"Okay, well I can tell you that Mat was in and out of trouble for the last couple of years, especially after he dropped out of school. He had done a bit of burglary and then went on to sell a bit of weed and that. About a year ago, he told me that he was running with some big league players, but he was very secretive and wouldn't tell me who they were."

"Did he tell you anything about them?"

"Only that they wouldn't think twice about heavy stuff if he stepped out of line. He was into good money and wanted to take the risk. Poor bugger. The risk didn't pay off."

"And you think they killed him? Why?"

"I don't know. I presume they were paramilitaries from one side or another and there was, maybe, some kind of feud. What I can tell you is that he was part of a huge cocaine racket. He always had bags of the stuff and he'd just give it away and splash it around at parties."

"Anything else?"

He looked disappointed that I wasn't more impressed with his information.

"No, not really, but that's more than I told the police. I never told anyone about all the coke. Also, there's a few of his friends I could talk to and I bet I could get at least one name for you at a push. You interested?"

"I would be, yeah, but it would need to be more concrete than what you gave me today. Keep that money, we'll say it'll pay towards your expenses and if you get me a name I'll pay you some more."

"Alright, yeah," he said, a childlike smile appearing on his lips. "I'll get you a name, Mr. Caskey."

***

It didn't all quite make sense yet. I slept on it. I slept on it pretty late and took an early afternoon run in the car over to the Titanic Quarter. I passed the Odyssey Arena and the Titanic Signature Building, a state of the art museum in the shape of Titanic's hull. I left my car in the car park behind the Holiday Inn, a close walk to the Public Records office. I had a smoke outside and let the sun warm my face as I looked out towards Belfast Lough and two large fishing boats docking up. I threw the butt down and headed inside. It was a long shot, but I was hoping there might be something useful I could find here. Once I had located the right area and paid my fifteen pounds for photocopies, I took my report on Screaming Tree. You could get information on nearly any organisation, but it would be limited unless additional information had been released in the public interest or after a granted request. The department seemed very efficient and the appearance of a corporate and highly organised library quite appealed to me. I took my documents down the road to the coffee shop in the Titanic Museum. I got a sandwich and a coke. I resisted the urge to ask for extra ice in my coke or iceberg in my sandwich. The report was much like I had expected. Various information was there that I had already found on the net, though more detailed. Screaming Tree had been set up in 2006 in Belfast, etc. etc. Some was more useful though. The CEO was registered as a J. Cantrell. It was a Limited Company and the records showed a steady growth in profit through its time in existence. The last three years saw a significant spike and a continuing upward trajectory. There was nothing here to give me a firm link to Sean's Trust and certainly not to the teenager. I had to check though. I finished my lunch and walked back to the car.

***

I headed back onto the bypass and pack through town. I left my car, somewhat illegally parked, up a curb behind the University and the new library complex. Apparently, they have a new "Narnia room" type of set up as a tribute to C.S. Lewis in an ornate reading room overlooking University Square. Maybe they'll add a "Billy Chapman" type room in a couple of years, too.

It was a dry and mild afternoon with little breeze. I strolled through the side gate to Botanic and walked around the perimeter. It's a nice old park, right in the hub of Queen's. I wolfed a couple of cigarettes and startled a few students having a cheeky joint outside The Ulster Museum on the far side of the trees. I might have done that a bit on purpose. The museum is one, ugly building like an unimaginative child has tried making a castle out of grey Dupelo blocks. I called into the café, on the ground floor of the museum, and took out a filter coffee and caramel square for the remainder of my walk. I had forgotten my loyalty card that pissed me off, but I took a couple of extra sugars for my pocket to make me feel better. I stopped at a group of benches beside the huge, Victorian glass house filled with exotic plants and flowers. I hunched over and stared at some browning leaves, picturing that kid with the football for a moment. I thought about The Causeway too and what Billy would find there if he returned. I just drifted.

"Are you okay, love?"

The voice startled me and I had the sudden realisation that I had been sitting there for quite some time.

"Yes, yes I'm fine," I replied, looking up in a haze. Maybe I had inhaled some of that joint. A plump lady in her fifties with an old-fashioned, navy rain coat looked down at me. Her face looked kind, but it was hard to tell as it was full of slap.

She smiled thinly. "That's good, just checking." She hesitated and then took a step closer. "It's just you were talking to yourself a little there," she added, sheepishly.

"Oh, sorry, I must do that sometimes. No, no I'm fine," I said, standing up. "Thanks though," I offered, walking off back towards the gates. The walk hadn't cleared my head much and I felt uneasy for the rest of the day. You know when you have a wee afternoon nap and you think you're going to feel great? You get all sleepy, go over and then wake up feeling fucking shite? It was a bit like that.

After vegging for the early evening in front of shite-like EastEnders, with a ten deck and a few coffees, I went out. I needed out. It was on these kind of nights that my mind would wander and I'd dwell and think about her and what happened. I still couldn't let myself do that. I took the car down to near The Oval and got out for a walk. I suppose I was looking for some "inspiration" from my muse! It was a pleasant night, a T-shirt and flannel shirt was enough to keep my arms warm. I walked along Dee Street and up towards Belmont, trying to take in the cranes and noises and smells as if I hadn't experienced them over and over since childhood. As I approached the top of the hill, the newly painted Strand Cinema greeted me. It was a sympathetic, light blue fitting in with the Art Deco design. I glanced at the backlit ads for their showings and sparked a cigarette. Almost all looked terrible - chick flicks, a no brain actioner, a weepy based on a sad novel. But, there was one contender, showing as part of one of the many arts festivals that Belfast now boasts; "Spellbound." A lesser celebrated Hitchcock movie from 1945. Gregory Peck stars as a man impersonating a psychiatrist who may also be a murderer. The problem is he doesn't know who he actually is, or what he's done, because of amnesia. I hadn't watched it in years and I was sold. Maybe it would help with period detail for my story, too. I threw my smoke down and rushed on in to make sure I caught the start. It had been a long time since I had been to the cinema. The last time probably had been in The Strand and with... well, now I was on my own. And, it wasn't so bad. The cinema was almost full. I had missed the communal atmosphere of going to a film, the crunch of the popcorn and my slushie giving me friggen brain freeze.

***

Two hours later, I was back on the street and hungry for a smoke. I ambled in the direction of my car, the crowd gradually disintegrating into different directions, car doors banging shut. I had enjoyed the film; probably all the more for the unexpected nature of an impromptu trip to the flicks. As I neared the bottom of the hill, and the start of the estate, the street became empty aside from me and one other. The street lights were fewer at this end and I couldn't see the figure properly at first as it appeared to stagger towards me. When I was a few paces away, I tensed my body, recognising the stubborn leer of an angry drunk.

"Hey ya," he shouted abruptly.

I stopped a metre away and took a pace to the side. I eyed him - a stocky type, a bit short and always annoyed by it. He looked rough and his skin was grey and his eyes bloodshot. I didn't speak and waited for him to go by. I didn't feel intimidated by a wee hard nut like him, especially after that post-cinema, "I'm a superhero too" feeling.

"What're ya looking at ya wee prick?" he slurred, jabbing his finger in the air.

"Fuck away off," I said, dryly and went to move past him.

He surprised me at his ability for swift action and lunged at me, shouting, "Fenian bastard!"

Instincts kicked in and I managed to push him back. Then my right arm swung back, I released it and my fist crunched into his jaw. He went down like a sack of shite, dazed but not badly hurt. I walked on, proudly, and tried not to hold my throbbing hand too obviously.

The next morning my friend in the pub, and minor illegal activity business, gave me a call. He had seemingly become impatient with my progress and contacted those that he paid so handsomely for first rate protection. They asserted that neither they, nor paramilitaries from the other side were responsible for the stabbing or for the liquor theft job. The dead teenager was indeed heavily mixed up in the local, cocaine business with some other hoods who kept themselves fairly under the radars. The word was that they didn't approve of this young man's growing sideline in other various criminal activities. His services were no longer required.

The day had started with some activity for a change, so I thought I'd strike while the iron was lukewarm. I worked up my case and made myself a few notes, got my shit together as they say. I horsed down a chili chicken sandwich and a homemade Starbucks before fixing to visit Jim. I got to Lisburn for one thirty and to the substantial former farm house on the outskirts. It stood on a three-acre plot and my pal Tim had lived there since being a kid. The walls could do with a paint job of their greying render and some new pebbledash painted on, but it had a charm. Jim had long since sold off most of the land that set him up to be comfortable. It was small change to Tim, due to his MS that had recently deteriorated to a point where he had started using the wheelchair at times.

"Come on in Brian, get your feet up and have a drink," he said, holding onto the door to steady himself.

"Tim, it's been a while. I'm sorry I haven't come for a bit."

I shook his hand, sensing the weakening in his grip, also noticing the hair on his wrist now greying like the thin moss left on his head.

"Not at all, you're here now," he said, leading me into the living room, through a half-lit musty corridor, with décor your Aunt Doris would be proud of. He headed straight for his chair and signaled me to go over to the drinks table. He eased into position beside his small, wooden coffee table having necessities in hand; his cigarettes, T.V remote, mobile phone and a few magazines.

"So things okay really?" Tim asked, sensitively after we had finished a round of small talk. We had sank a few whiskeys too.

"Yeah, like I was saying, I have this case and I'm gonna give it a good shot."

"Good, good, well if I can be any help with it just let me know."

I had thought I probably would talk to Tim properly about it. We had worked on the force together and he was a smart guy. But, for some reason, I wanted to keep it distant. I knew what I wanted to do anyway.

"So, what's this shit we're listening to," I asked, pointing with my cigarette to the record player.

"This 'shit' is ESP," Tim answered, with a bantering grimace.

"Oh, well I'm not psychic, so that means nothing to me."

"Bloody Miles Davis," he barked. "Amazing album. Herbie and Wayne Shorter and those guys, just before the electrics came in." He pulled out a spliff from his faded Barbour cardigan and lit it up.

"Those guys were pretty cool."

"You know Miles went up to a leader of a band once and whispered in his ear... 'I'm gonna steal your fucking bass player,' and he did. Crazy cats, those guys, there's all sorts of stories. But man, could they play."

"Fair enough, not bad," I admitted, "I know a bit of Herbie and that, more a fusion kind of a guy me."

"Haha, yeah right, you don't know your be-bop from your swing, you still loving all your grunge crap?"

"You still smoking that crap?" I retorted.

"Medicinal."

I had a draw or two, but as usual it didn't agree with me.

Chapter Twenty-Five

The train was slow and there were plenty of security checks. Dublin's only a hundred miles away from Belfast, but it took a good chunk of the day to get there. The train had been the late morning one and I only got into Connolly station a few hours before dinner. I enjoyed the journey down, passing rural communities and a few small towns. It was dry and it felt pleasant inside the rail car. The click... clack and the smoky whisps past the window were a nice addition to my senses. I had a flask of coffee with me and a sandwich to keep body and soul together, too. Of course, I also had copious cigarettes. The scenery was beautiful and it was no wonder that we're called the Emerald Isle. I thought about the train journey I had made up to the Causeway and those strange few days that had followed. I had been to almost the length of the island in the last few weeks and felt like I had joined Fosset's circus. I don't know why my thoughts kept turning to Mary McKenzie and the regret that I had left the Causeway so suddenly. I finished my sandwich after we passed over The Boyne and there were no Dutch kings in sight. I doubt there would have been one particularly visible in 1690 either. I opened my copy of Dubliners; I hadn't read any Joyce since he had died earlier that year and it seemed a fitting time to read a few of his short stories to pass the time. I only got through two before my eyes grew heavy and I let the book drop in my lap. It had been a heavy couple of weeks.

***

I stepped onto the platform and pulled my case off me. I had woken with a jolt and was a little bit disorientated. There was quite the hubbub around me but it was strange not seeing anyone in uniform. I joined the hustle of commuters heading towards the gates; businessmen, a few families and one fella trailing a double bass. When we got through security, and into the huge terminal, he greeted a guy with a sax. Almost immediately they broke into a swing standard and they sure could swing. I stopped and listened and smoked another cigarette. When I through a few pennies into their open case I received a gracious nod. When they saw it was sterling I'm nearly sure they both shot me a surly look. As I walked around the city I thought I got a few more looks when people heard my accent. As far I was concerned we were all Irish. It's just that I saw myself as British as well. For the most part, though, everyone I met was friendly. Many seemed drunk, too. In the first bar I went into everyone was. I spent a few hours carrying out some research. This involved drinks and smokes and some "fiddly dee" music. I like Irish traditional a lot and there were some talented guys all over the city. Most importantly, I asked a lot of questions about Kantian Park. Most people hadn't heard of it but, gradually, I met some who knew a few little bits and then some who even had former friends that lived there. The craic was mighty as they say. Most of the inebriated, after accepting a drink or three, from me said how much they loved The North. They also tended to say something along the lines of how if it was up to them they would be fighting Hitler alongside us and seemed to mean it, too. Afternoon turned to evening and then slipped into a warm night. I padded around the city centre with my sleeves rolled up, case in one hand and suit jacket in the other. I had found out The Kantian movement had seemingly been founded on the principles of the philosopher Immanuel Kant. Self-sufficient communities had been set up in a few dozen sites throughout Europe over the following three decades. This one had been going only a few years before the war and was viewed with a large dose of Dublin suspicion. They called themselves Scientific Christians and had a considerable plot, using the *land for agriculture and animal farming. Other than that I knew nothing about them; certainly no obvious connections to Nazi spies.*

I crossed over the Liffey and walked about the Temple Bar quarter. The architecture was impressive and the city had a pleasant hum in the evening time; much preferable to a bomber engine. The recent bombing hadn't touched the city centre. It was hard to contrast it fairly to Belfast centre when even Belfast City Hall had part of its roof blown to pieces. I always liked Temple Bar and crawled into a few more pubs in between watching some street performers. As it got closer towards closing time those hitting the cobbles weren't anywhere near as friendly or, quite frankly, very much less than down right sinister. There were scowls and mutterings and even a growl. I headed to my hotel, dragging my case one last time. I was quite sozzled, but handling it okay. The Gresham Hotel was the old dame of Dublin. It had been there since the early 1800s and had an old world charm. I was afforded a warm welcome I was unused to in the North, where people seemed to sum up how much you were worth as soon as they shook your hand. I took in the grand reception area and the multitude of staff before I was shown up to my room. I kind of missed Maggie though. Before I closed my eyes on the huge and back massaging bed, my mind floated towards Kantian Park.

***

Breakfast was fine but it was no Ulster. The Bewleys coffee was good though. I decided to make one morning stop before going in search of the community. I took the tram across the city and was distracted by craving a large drink of water. My mouth was dry and my stomach felt like it had about six dinners in it after all the stodgy Guinness I had consumed the night before. In fairness it had been the creamiest stout I have ever tasted and I had had a bit much. I got off near the GPO where the Rising had been during the last World War and where it kicked off a new civil war. I stopped and had a look around the outside. The twentieth century had been bloody most places so far and Ireland had been saturated. It took me a while to find the local office of Bushmills Whiskey, Ltd. It was a few streets off the bustling O'Connell Street. I had been thinking about the Frank McKenzie case almost as much as Laura's. I knew I owed her my full concentration and time could still be of the essence. If I had a quick word with Mr. Dufferin, the owner, then I thought I could perhaps put my mind to rest. I hadn't found much of suspicion, that was true, but the nature of my quitting the Causeway had left it all quite unresolved in my head. I had my doubts over something a little fishy going on with the company and I hoped if I could meet Mr. Dufferin, then I might be satisfied. There was a small, metal gray sign on the wall of the Georgian, terrace office. It was beside the black door, up three steps from the path. I went through the door and into a small, waiting area segregated from a working office by a counter and glass window. A tall man got up from his desk on the other side and took off his glasses. He walked across and opened up the hatch. He was thin and around thirty with a North Dublin lilt. He looked like a serious sort, but offered a thin smile.

"Good morning to you, how I can I help you?"

"Hello, the name's Chapman, I don't have an appointment but I was hoping to arrange one for today if possible."

"That may be possible," he responded, with slight irritation, "What is the nature of your business and who is it you would like to see? Most of us in this office are in finance and the importing of produce to the Republic. If you are wishing to talk about sales business I'm afraid we wouldn't be much help to you. That's all handled up north."

"I was hoping to meet very briefly with Mr. Dufferin, if possible, today or tomorrow."

"Oh," he said, with surprise. "He isn't here. Mr. Dufferin hasn't been to this office since it was first set up several years ago. We wouldn't be expecting him either, at this time."

I held on to the counter lightly and pressed. "It's just that I was at your Head Office and was informed Mr. Dufferin had been working out of this office for several months."

"I'm sorry," he said, with a shrug. "You have been misinformed, or mistaken, Mr. Dufferin has not been here."

As I walked down the steps again, away from the smart row of houses turned offices, I smiled. I'm not sure why. I knew there was another case to get back to and, somehow, I felt some sense of satisfaction in that. I knew that I would let it wait until the other business was settled. Maybe I was just glad that I'd be sure now of seeing Mary McKenzie again.

***

I couldn't get a train, bus or tram to leave me anywhere near Kantian Park. It was a good bit outside of Dublin following the coast out in the general direction of Bray. The train took me a little of the way and then I was on foot. I didn't mind much. It was a clear day and the breeze off the Irish Sea made a walk through a stretch of countryside very pleasant. The last time I had been out in this kind of rolling countryside was in France and that was very different. I had phoned Kantian Park from my hotel that morning and they were expecting me. They were used to giving strangers directions that were pretty easy to follow. It wasn't a case of turn right at the third tree on the left; or even the "terd tee" as they enunciated down in these parts. They had put up a few sign posts on the way and it gave me time to think about my plan. I had told them my real name because they said that anyone registered, even for the day, *had to be signed in and accounted for. I said that I was not long back from war and was looking for God and a bit of hope. Half of it was probably true. I soon could see where the community was situated as I approached over a small incline. I could make out a little, wooden hut and a church a few hundred yards away. I sat down on some rocks and had a smoke and a bacon bap I had saved from breakfast, wrapped in my trouser pocket. I put my jacket back on and felt optimistic as I approached the open, wooden gates. I looked around the outside of the hut and the small, granite church. Both were locked and a pleasant breeze cooled my skin as I started down the rough path through a thin stretch of forest. I could hear birdsong and the lapping of the sea close by. I could see why people might want to come here. If there had been rattlesnakes and tigers in Ireland this would still have been much preferable to the chaos of my city. After a few hundred yards the path meandered into a clearing and I could hear some relaxed sounding chatter and the clip... clip of people gardening. I went on and could see an immature garden landscaped carefully in front of five or six small, brick houses. There were some young trees, newly planted, various shrubs and a new flowering of rose bushes. It would be something special when it was finished and had a chance to grow for a couple of seasons. There were seven or eight members throughout the gardens working with clippers, shears and rakes. A lady, in her early forties, with a floppy hat and pink summer dress got up from kneeling at some bluebells. They were just going over and needed taken up.*

"Hello," she said, softly as she walked towards me. She had a pretty, unassuming face.

"Hello. This is some place you have here."

She smiled sweetly and her face was kind.

"Thank you, we like to think so. Are you Mr. Chapman?"

She stretched out her toned brown arm and I shook her hand.

"Yes, pleased to meet you."

"I'm Margaret. I'm one of the circuit stewards here. Let me show you around."

"I appreciate you letting me come and see the place and I hope, maybe in the future, I might end up joining the group here."

"I hope so too, Mr. Chapman. God has a plan for all of us. In these worrying times, it's important to let the mind have peace and you will find it can here."

She nodded to some of the gardeners and a few murmured "Hello" and "God's blessings" to me as we walked through the garden towards the group of houses.

"This is the centre of our community, though the church you would have passed is the heart. We all live together in these houses and we are building more down by the beach you can see," she gestured over a stone wall to a grassy patch raised a little above the coast.

"How long have you lived here yourself?" I asked her, lighting up a smoke.

She winced. "I'm sorry but if you were to join us there are certain habits you would have to leave behind."

"Oh, I'm sorry," I lied, and I didn't think my cover could stretch to me not having a smoke the rest of the day.

"It's alright Mr. Chapman. Feel free." She gave a kindly smile and started to lead us on. "I have been here since the beginning. There were only a few of us then; now we are forty eight and before the war we would have had frequent volunteers staying with us for part of the year."

I lit up like a naughty school boy and exhaled to the side. "That's very interesting. Are there many here from overseas too then now?"

"Yes, we are an international community. There are no politics here. We have, in our community, many from all

over Europe and our leader was originally from the United States."

"I have wanted to visit a Kantian community for a long time but I, unfortunately, still don't know as much as I would like to."

She patted my arm and led me along the coastal path towards a few, small, l fishing boats. "Do not worry, we have plenty of time to share a great deal with you. Sometimes a still tongue makes a happy life," she paused. "You know, of course, that we centre our teachings on those of Immanuel Kant. I will give you some of our literature to take with you and I have arranged for you to have a few minutes with our great leader here, Layne Dulli. Layne was the first to found a community here in Ireland. Of course, we are very much a part of the greater mission, but we are also quite our own entity. We see ourselves as another sect of Christianity you understand. Our central ethos is based on Kant's Critique of Pure Reason and his instruction to 'never treat a man as a means to end, but a means in oneself'."

"This is a very beautiful and peaceful place," I responded, and quite meant it. I would never have bought their whole shtick, but I didn't see anything too fishy about the place. They were probably just some well-intentioned bohemians and good luck to them, I thought.

"Mr. Chapman, this is Davy our chief builder and engineer," she said, as we walked towards a man getting out of a beached boat, fiddling with some fishing nets.

"Hello, Conas atá tú?" he said, with a careful reserve. He spoke it with a thick brogue. He couldn't have been more than five and a half foot, stocky but not fat, with a face like a half baked potato. He had small and sharp brown eyes and a thin crop of black hair.

"Pleased to meet you. I was telling your friend here what an incredible place you all live in."

"We like to think so," he said, and glancing over towards a small, stable courtyard out to the left of us. We all chatted quite formally as we walked towards the barns, now converted into Layne Dulli's quarters and offices.

"I must get back now, Mr. Chapman, Davy will see you inside and I'll meet you afterwards to register your interest properly. We will endeavour to get some of the formalities out of the way," she said, as we stopped at the recently, constructed doorway leading into the first barn.

"Thank you, again, for your time. I will see you later on then," I replied, shaking her hand gently.

"Gwan ahead," Davy said, a little coldly but trying not to.

"Thanks," I said, as I opened the door and found a surprisingly less modest interior. The building had been totally renovated and been done so with a lot of skill.

"It's a grand job isn't it," Davy said, a touch more enthusiastically. "Some of our colleagues from Italy did most of the design and craftsmanship. Have a seat over there."

I sat down on a cushioned, wooden chair as he disappeared into a room to the left. There was a staircase to the front of me leading up to a wooden platform and, I presumed, Dulli's upstairs quarters. The hall I was in was open plan and large. There was a huge table at the far end of the rectangular room, across newly sanded floors and overlooking a large, glass window. It looked out to the sea where there was a lighthouse out in the distance, on a small island reminding there was an outside world. Davy came back after a few minutes and said I could go into Dulli's office. He closed the door behind me.

"Ahh, Mr. Chapman, God's rich blessings," Dulli said, getting up from his oak desk. The room was a smaller and an even more elaborate microcosm of the outside hall complete with desk, window and view.

"*Good to meet you, I appreciate your seeing me. I am sure you are very busy*"

"*Please, have a seat, come on now, in you come,*" he said, eagerly grabbing my hand and almost leading me to a large, reclining chair at the other side of his desk. He poured a cola for us both out of a large, glass bottle.

"*Something of home Mr. Chapman and refreshing on a beautiful, and warm, afternoon like we have today, I think.*"

He was a tall and slender, handsome looking man in his mid-forties with a good head of jet, black hair. He had a twang in his voice with an occasional Irish lilt and an overall, velvety texture. With hindsight he would remind you of Jimmy Stewart.

"*Well sir, I just wanted to meet you briefly before you go because I know that you must rely on limited transport to get you home this fine day. Of course, the offer still remains if you would like to avail of our hospitality for a night or two; it would be our pleasure.*"

"*No, but thank you, Mr. Dulli. That is most generous. I have some urgent family matters to attend to tomorrow, but I do hope to return as a resident in the future if that becomes mutually agreeable.*"

"*Tremendous, tremendous,*" he said, jovially. "*I hope so too.*" He looked towards me a little more seriously and offered a wave with his hand after swigging some Coke. "*You understand that we will have to look at your application, but that really should just be a formality. Also, you realise, I trust, that anyone joining the community must agree to work as a community member wherever we see fit. We are quite self-sufficient and proud of that fact; but all must sow who also reaps.*"

"*Yes, of course,*" I said, trying to continue with my fawned enthusiasm that was beginning to wane. "*I would only be too happy.*"

"Good, good, that's swell then. We would love to have a patriot, such as yourself, counted in our number. I believe you would be a welcomed addition and could bring much glory to the Lord here."

We finished our drinks and, after he gave me some more of the community jargon, wrapped up our conversation. I was moved out of the room on a wave of bluster, and apparent unwavering belief in Kantian Park from Dulli, as he talked ten to the dozen of all his plans for the future. I didn't really have time to reflect on our meeting before I was ushered out by him. Then, it seemed to work on some other new converts or whatever. Margaret was back pretty much on cue and she then ushered me into the second barn. It wasn't finished to the same standard and looked more like a telegraph office not long setup in the Wild West. I was brought into a small room with a few filing cabinets, desk and some stationary. I couldn't be sure, but Margaret appeared a little standoffish now; though her words were friendly enough.

"So, let's make a start then," she said, as we sat at the desk together. She had two ledgers in front of her and a black file. "We will need a current passport and one other form of identification. A bill of some description with your address would suffice, will that be a problem?"

"No, not at all, I have everything here," I said, as I lifted out my documents from my bag.

"I apologise that our system is so detailed, but it is all to the glory of God."

We talked at length or, rather, I did as she took copious notes and examined my papers.

"I'm sorry to interrupt you both," a young girl said, in cooking whites after knocking and entering. "But the long distance phone call you were expecting has come through."

"Oh, thank you," Margaret replied, thoughtfully closing both ledgers. "I will be with you, presently."

She got up swiftly and walked to the door. "Mr. Chapman, you must excuse me. I apologise again that this process is quite laborious and I appreciate that you must leave shortly. I will be only a few minutes."

"That is no problem at all, take your time," I replied, sensing her distraction. It pricked my interest at the same time. I could wonder a year and a night what was going on in this place exactly but I didn't have the time. I had two cases that needed finishing and the Nazis at our door besides. I knew there was at least an opportunity to get some information I needed for the girl and that was all that mattered. For good or bad, I was the only one could find Mrs Morris some answers.

They left together and closed the door. I listened carefully to hear their steps walk away and then the outside door closed. I lost the sound of their steps as they moved from gravel to lawn. I moved swiftly around the table, checking that no one was outside through the small window. I loosened my shirt at the top where my neck had started to perspire. My fingers were clammy and I rubbed them on my loosened shirt. I opened both ledgers at once and scrolled through them, getting about halfway and then flicking through the file a few pages. There were meticulous notes on members of the community and various referrals for new recruits. There were passport numbers, work skill dossiers and financial records. I was rushed and didn't have the time to try and digest it all. I needed one tangible detail, one nugget. I got to the last section of the black file. These pages contained general information on passports, army records and immigration reports. Gradually, though, an alarm started ringing way down in my stomach, and then straight up into my cranium. There was something starting to form in the creative part of my brain that hadn't been soaked over the years like sherry casks. It was a typed list of names with ticks in pencil beside all of the names but one. It was a document from the home office listing immigrants settling in Eire and then moving to Northern Ireland. There was one name circled in pencil and beside it a few asterisks. I wondered if it was the same pencil that had first led me to this place. The name I certainly knew. Purposeful footsteps came down the hall; at least two sets of feet. I ripped the page out, instinctively, and stuffed it into my pocket. The door swung open, heavily, and Davy came in with rent a mob. Rent a mob was tall, tanned and mean; like Al Capone put through a toaster.

"What are you doing," Davy asked, firmly though a little out of breath.

"Just getting some air," I answered, after stepping towards the window before they had entered.

"Something has come up and we will not have the opportunity to finish your paperwork today," he said, trying to flip into a bank clerk style. He would have fitted better at the other end from a teller with a mask over his face.

"Oh, I hope that won't affect my application."

"No, not at all," he said, now like we were old sea buddies again. "We can finish that up later. It is just that we have this little problem and we'll have to end the visit there."

"That's fine, I would be needing to get to my bus soon, thank you again for the hospitality," I said, eager to get out of there, too. I didn't start to get a normal pulse back until I was walking in the evening sun, out of sight from Kantian Park. Only once I was safely on my bus did I look at the sheet again. I didn't much care who exactly was mixed up in what, I only cared about the name. The name on the list was Martineau.

Chapter Twenty-Six

I went into town in the afternoon. I had a few things to do, but I also wanted to check out where Screaming Tree had their offices. I circled around the one way system, past the back of the city hall twice to see where it was. I clocked it and felt better to know where it lay especially if I might end up paying them a visit sometime. I parked around at the multi-story at In-Shops up on the top floor. There was a good view of some of older Belfast and the old, cobbled part of the Cathedral Quarter. I looked their number up on my phone, took a second to compose myself and then rang it.

"Hello, Screaming Tree, how may I help you?"

"Hello, yes, my name is Mark Turner and I am phoning from Belfast Assisted Living Trust."

"Yes, how can I help," asked the friendly and professional sounding girl on the other end.

"We are a charity and I am looking at a number of companies to see who would best be suited to deal with our marketing and commercial needs."

"Yes, we could certainly help with that."

"That's good. Yes, I am aware of the good reputation your organisation has. I would be wanting to arrange a consultation, to see what you can offer."

"That would be no problem at all. I could schedule that for when suits you."

"Could I just check? Aren't you the company who has done a great job with the corporate aspects of Sean's Trust?"

A moment of sudden silence follow then she spoke.

"I'm sorry what was that?"

"I said, isn't it right you oversee publicity matters for Sean's Trust?"

"No, that is not us," she said firmly. "They are not one of our clients. Now," she said, again more breezily. "When would be convenient for you to come in, or we could come to you?"

"Thanks, but I'll come back to you. I just need to look at my schedule."

I cut the line. I had a wee ponder, then locked up the car and hopped into the lift. I needed a string for my acoustic guitar so I thought I'd go for that first before I forgot about it. This whole Sean's Trust thing was certainly getting interesting. I headed up Royal Avenue and past all the main shopping areas. Castle Court and Victoria Square are the two big malls and I avoid them like the plague. I turned up right at the front of City Hall to head up Wellington to Matchetts Music. The buzzer chirped as I went in, announcing my arrival to the three or four other customers and the one salesman. He had dreads, an affectation and a chain on his jeans pockets so I presumed he worked there. I'd also wager he was vegan. I don't think I had been in a music shop for a couple of years, but slotted into my normal routine of looking at all the guitars, then the amps, then the music books. When I was halfway between the shitty Squires and the really not shitty Gretschs, 'Dreads' came over to me.

"You okay there man?" he asked, quietly, almost conspiratorially.

"Yeah, cheers, just looking" I said.

"Okay," he responded, with a huffy voice and flick of a dread.

I fucking hate the twats who work in music shops. *You're not a rock star and you're also not a top salesman for BMW. Your work mainly involves selling shitty guitars to children and plectrums to everyone else.* I carried on with my perusing and then went up to the counter to get my string.

"Hi," Dreads said, with a forced smile.

"Could I have a high E string please, Ernie Ball nines if possible?

"You just want one string?" he asked.

"Yes."

"We don't do that."

"You don't sell strings?"

"We don't sell singles."

I looked past him at the rows of packs and considered this.

"But I only broke one string, I don't need the rest."

"We only sell sets of strings. And when you break a string, you should replace them all."

My face I'm sure was tripped. I didn't say anything for a second, probably for the best.

"Do you want the pack of nines?"

I held it together.

"Yeah, please, how much?"

I pulled my wallet out of my back pocket.

"It's seven ninety-nine."

"For fuck sake."

I cooled off on my walk back towards the Cathedral Quarter. It was my main reason for going into town that day. I was going to visit the Northern Ireland War Memorial. I hadn't been before and from their website it looked like there should be lots of good stuff for my story. The map on my phone hadn't been too clear but, after finding a street map, I soon located Memorial House. It was a pretty ugly building to be honest. I had read that it had been built after the war on the ruins of a site devastated by the Blitz in tribute. Pity they hadn't made it look nicer. I went up to the door and sounded the buzzer.

"Hello, LGB Society," came a tinny voice.

"I'm sorry what?"

"LGB Society, can I help you?"

"Sorry, is this the War Memorial?"

"No, Lesbian, Gay, Bisexual Society."

"Oh," I said, trying not to sound like a stereotypical, prejudiced Ulsterman.

"It used to be here, they sold the building off, got moved a few years back. Don't worry, it happens a lot. You want Talbot Street, on down the bottom, just before Saint Anne's."

"Okay, cheers very much for your help."

I zigzagged again, this time towards the Cathedral and treated myself to a ciggie. I also allowed myself a wry smile. *What would my Grandfather have thought of selling off the War Memorial to the gays?*

I found it easy enough after that. It was a small museum, housed in a modern block with various other businesses scattered inside. I pressed the buzzer and the young guide let me in. He was by himself and gave me a quick spiel, then left me up to my own devices. The room was an open plan. I compared my guide sheet to what was in front of me. It seemed that the large memorials had been taken in whole from the old site to this one. On my right was a large, stained glass tribute to the sacrifice of those in the war with "We will Remember" etched simply across the bottom. There was an intricate, black marble mural in front of me representing the war in pictures and a bronze statue of a widow and her daughter to my left. I went slowly through the museum, reading every information panel carefully. I had brought my notebook and filled four or five sides. There were a lot of facts and figures I hadn't known, like in one night alone ninety-six thousand incendiaries were dropped on the city, twenty-six thousand men were in the Home Guard, eighteen hundred local girls became GI brides and Harland and Wolff had built one hundred and forty warships for the Allies. I'd have to weave some of this into the story. I spent a pleasant hour or so there and took away a few of their brochures with more information on them. It all brought it home how the period shouldn't be treated lightly and it deserved to be still shown a reverence. I walked back to the car feeling sombre, but stimulated.

I had a coffee in Café Nero and Googled "Screaming Tree" some more, specifically to see what the boss Mr. Cantrell looked like. I treated myself to some cappuccino cake when my laptop died. I found a picture of him that was good before that and felt a tinge of excitement as I ingested my double caffeine hit.

***

I had collected my car and then drove to the corner behind City Hall where their office was. I parked up on a double yellow, but was lucky and no one tried moving me on. It was four thirty so I sat and waited. From around a quarter past five, people began to exit the building. Just before six, I clocked Cantrell. He was average height, middle aged and wearing a light black coat over his grey suit. I watched as he turned the corner and walked in the direction of Shaftesbury Square. I started up the engine and pulled into the slow traffic. The rush hour, bumper to bumper suited me and I managed to keep a close distance behind without drawing any attention. He went past the Ulster Hall and crossed over next to the BBC. He was heading for the multi-story. I pulled into the side street and waited. I inspected each car tensely as they left and spotted Cantrell driving his silver, Audi estate car. He swung out towards the Ormeau Road and I pulled into the traffic two cars behind. In my early days, in the RUC, tailing was something I picked up quickly and quite enjoyed. I continued like this past the Albert Clock and onto the bypass. It was slow and took us half an hour to get to Holywood. He turned off down towards the bay and I followed suit, the only other car to do so. I drove on past as he turned into a large driveway with big, black gates and looking in as I passed to see a modern, large, red brick house detached with double garage. I drove on for five minutes before doubling back. I idled to a stop across the road and just before his house. I had a good view of the drive, but was partly concealed by the trees lined along the footpath. As darkness was coming, I could slump down and the car look empty. I settled myself to be in for a wait. I realised I already wanted a piss. It's probably the knowing that you can't. I've never been a fan of stakeouts. I put the radio on low and was still feeling ripples of adrenaline. I did for the first hour or two anyway. By the time it got to ten I was really fucking bored and not one person had arrived or left. I decided I wasn't going to get far like this and split. On the way home I stopped at The Hot Spot picking up a Hawaiian burger and a gravy chip. I felt a fair amount of satisfaction as I tucked into them back at my flat. That night, I decided I would have to take a more direct approach. I had another nightmare, but turned over and went straight back to sleep.

***

I had other things to do the next day and was glad to give myself a bit of perspective. It was still buzzing about my head, but the case could wait a day of two. I had been putting off paying some bills and sat at the kitchen counter for half the morning. I probably should have started with the situation with my mortgage, but I decided to put off that more troubling issue for a bit longer. Three cups of coffee later and I had gone through everything, discarded the junk, written three cheques and made two phone calls. It was mostly all in hand and I felt better for it. Occasionally, I need a day to just focus on this kind of boring shit. I then did some spring cleaning. It was really just a tip of the iceberg thing; empty the overflowing bins, wipe some of the layers of food and dirt off the counter, clean the piss off the bathroom floor. I was on a roll. I headed out to Tesco and stocked up on all the big things that I hated shopping for - washing tablets, toilet rolls etc. It was late afternoon by the time I was done and I fixed myself a chicken curry and rice, using a new jar of "chip shop" curry sauce. I felt good. I hadn't drank all day and had smoked only four or five cigs. I decided to go into the city centre for a midweek drink. It's something I rarely did. I showered, changed and then walked round to the train station. When I got to Botanic, it was chucking it down. I bolted next door to have one in the Empire before walking further in. The Empire is a great old venue. It used to be a church and has two separate parts: one up, one down. The upstairs is more for concerts and downstairs for everything else. I walked down the steps, quickly, and entered the bar. It was darker than the dusk outside. The football had just finished and there were a lot of groups leaving. Over in the corner a guy in his early twenties was setting up a microphone beside his acoustic guitar. He had a nice looking Lowden. The Guinness is good in The Empire and I ordered a pint of stout and positioned my frame on the bar where I could see the little stage and also the TV. I stayed to hear a couple of songs and they weren't bad. The guy could sing. He was playing his own stuff I think and it was quite good. There was a small crowd and some seemed to know him. There was the familiar overexertion of applause someone gets at local gigs from their friends and family. Off to the side was a middle aged man with a thick, black beard. He was sitting with a sketch book, drawing the image of this young man. He seemed to know the sound guy well, probably a regular addition to the session here. I was enjoying myself, but felt like I wanted to hear a band. I went out for a smoke and the rain had eased to only a drip. I pulled the hoodie up that was under my black jacket as I set off. I walked down Shaftesbury Square in the general direction of the centre, past all the fast food places and cafés. As I came to the next group of bars, I kept a look out for any signs of live music. It was nearly ten and things should have started up by then.

I approached Auntie Annie's and could hear the sound of a miked up bass drum and the drone of muffled guitars. The two bouncers eyed me suspiciously as I had a look at the poster on the wall outside. I didn't take it personally. There are so many prick bouncers in Belfast, it's nuts. A band by the name of Spun were playing, it was a CD launch for their new album, with a nice wee quote from Hotpress Magazine on the poster. I paid the first bouncer the three quid and he grunted that the gig was upstairs. I headed up and the music washed around the echoey stair case. When I opened the door, I had to side step to let a couple of pretty attractive, young girls past, both with a grungy kind of look going on. I approved. There was a crowd of fifty or sixty inside, filling out the space well between the bar and the three piece who were blasting out a slice of decent alternative rock. I pushed gently to get to the bar and got another Guinness and a whiskey chaser. The Guinness was alright, but a bit warmer than the Empire's. I listened to a couple of songs and enjoyed them. Mostly, it was a novelty to be out in a rock bar seeing a local band. I had done a lot of this in the past but that was even before I joined the police. Not the Sting guys. My mind wondered off to my story and I tried to think about where it would head to next. I'm not very good at planning out a plot and usually just see where it takes me. I kind of wanted to know where it would end up, though. Maybe I could just finish it mid-flow like Kafka. When the singer/guitarist started to speak, I realised they were pretty wasted. I couldn't quite make out what he said the song was called but I was distracted by the guitar anyway, trying to work out if it was a genuine Les Paul or one of the many copies that were floating around. Apparently, I wasn't the only one who couldn't hear him as a lanky man in his twenties beside me heckled loudly in a southern brogue,

"What's that you say? We can't hear you."

The singer turned his head and mumbled something that I think was "love is an anchor."

"What did you say- 'someone's a wanker?'" the southern guy shouted, outraged. He looked at me. "I don't believe it, someone's a fucking wanker."

He strode up to the stage and started hurling abuse at the singer and the band in general. They didn't seem at all phased, they were pissed anyway. Abruptly, Pebbles and Bam-Bam came roaring up the stairs and set upon the unsuspecting heckler. They dragged him out with a couple of discreet digs for good measure. The band went into "Love is an Anchor" without further introduction.

***

I lay in bed, smoking. I was sleepy and I knew I really shouldn't smoke there last thing at night. I was half cut, too. I had watched the end of the set and even stayed for a bit of the DJ. Now that I was home, back in my normal surroundings and somewhere that was not clean and tidy, but was much more clean and tidier than it had been, my thoughts returned to the case. I must have sat awake for a couple of hours, mulling everything over and working out what needed to be done.

The next afternoon, I think was a Wednesday, I stood on the corner of Civic Street and lit a cigarette out from a fresh pack of twenty. This was following my lunch time tablet and a can of full fat coke. After said lunch I walked up to the steps of Screaming Tree's Belfast office. It was in a lovely, old building in the square, around the back of City Hall, sharing with the Chamber of Commerce and a Starbucks. My confidence had almost abandoned me following a purposeful stroll from my car. I sucked it up and headed on inside.

"I'm sorry but Mr. Cantrell is not taking any meetings this afternoon."

"So he is in?" I pressed the young, attractive blonde on reception.

"Well yes, but he is not taking any calls or visitors I am afraid. If you would like to leave a message perhaps?" she asked, full of both professionalism and enthusiasm, only someone in their twenties still has.

I leaned in a little so none of the other people milling around the slick reception area could hear me.

"Tell him it's about the cocaine."

Her mouth dropped a little and then she composed herself and asked me to wait a minute. I was fairly certain she would be ringing security but she came back after no more than a few minutes and said to please come through. There was no waiting outside the headmaster's room today and I was ushered straight in to a large office. I sat in a comfortable leather chair opposite an imposing desk that was sparsely dressed with a notebook, telephone and writing box. There was a door to the right which looked to be an ensuite toilet and the white walls were filled with about a dozen, black framed covers of magazines and a few certificates for this and that. The room was flooded with natural light from the large, double window overlooking the bustling street and City Hall itself.

"Mr. Caskey," Cantrell greeted, rubbing his hands dry. "Can I offer you a drink?"

"Yes, I think we both ought to have a little whiskey."

He idled across to an opulent, modern, drinks cabinet and fixed us both a Black Bush. He was about forty five, lean with a dirty blonde head of hair, brushed back. He came round and sat down at his desk stretching to set a drink in front of us both.

"I think my secretary must have misheard you. What is your business?" he asked, coolly.

"Not if she heard that I wanted to talk about cocaine. And my business today is you."

"Please, make sense or I will have to ask security to see you out," he said, crisply.

"It's about how you have been shipping cocaine in from the south of France and selling it in Belfast. You're going to be in a lot of trouble."

"Preposterous, I have no idea what you're talking about."

"You helped set up a bogus charity as a cover for your narcotic activities which also involved a recent murder."

I took a long sip.

"That is ridiculous," he said, taking a sip of his own drink. "I have never heard such craziness."

I stumbled for a second, but found a little trickle of confidence left to continue. I hadn't got much to lose if I was wrong but, still, it was enough to send my head rushing slightly and my gut aching.

"Mr. Cantrell, this is fact and I have the proof to back it up," I bluffed. "You used the fake charity to launder the dirty money with all of the cash coming in from collection boxes and events. It probably was a good source of cash flow at times, I would imagine, too. You may leave most of the nasty stuff to others but you're in it right up to your neck."

He rose sharply. "You will get out of my office now, get out please," he said, in almost a quivering shout.

***

I got up and he walked around the side of the desk towards me. I headed slowly towards the door. I had him rattled and he knew it. His big tell had been not even asking who I was or what proof I had. I turned to have another last pop. I was greeted with a goggle-eyed man almost shrieking as he pushed me hard against the door. I could see some white powder on his gums. He didn't know what to do and I loosened my right arm and hit him a quarter punch to his mouth. He backed away and I hit him with a full left. He fell to the ground hard; old habits die hard and I kicked him in the stomach once for good measure. He wasn't much of a fighter and it made me feel like Barry McQuigan and Georgie Best rolled into one.

Chapter Twenty-Seven

The rest of the day was a blur and the train journey was, too, the following day. I didn't want to see another train again maybe more than another bomb. By evening, I was back in Belfast and at Great Victoria Street Station. There was a sweet smell of sulphur on the air. I got home and left off my bag, kicking my post out of the way. I washed up and went straight back out again. I got to University Square about nine o'clock. All of the houses were in darkness. I carefully went to the back of the History building and forced a small, kitchen window open only cracking slightly the lower panel of wood. I crept in awkwardly. I lit one of my matches and looked around. I didn't even know what I was looking for. I tiptoed upstairs and found Martineau's office was locked. I was past caring about formalities. I stepped back and kicked it hard beside the lock. It opened dramatically. I looked around and went in, leaving the door open. I searched everywhere, only lighting a candle to aid me. I searched aimlessly for half an hour, continually checking over my shoulder that no one was coming. I could find nothing that would offer any kind of further lead. I still hadn't any proof of any real value. I began to regret my hasty entrance when a voice from behind.

"Mr. Chapman," the voice said, quietly.

It sounded foreign, but not French... but German. I turned.

"Martineau," I said, dryly. A Smith and Wesson was pointed at me; I expected a Luger.

"Sit over there and keep your hands where I can see them," he instructed, in clipped tones.

"I preferred you when you were French," I offered.

I sat down and studied him. He was unlikely to kill me here, I thought. He perched on the desk like an eagle eyeing its breakfast.

"Where's the girl?" I asked, trying to stay calm.

"You shouldn't have gotten involved Chapman."

"Where is she?"

"She's dead, of course," he sighed.

My breath left me for a second. I held his gaze and realised he had quite a resemblance to Peter Lorre.

"The ransom was just for distraction then?"

"And for time." He looked to be examining me.

"She was on to your network then, was that it? I suppose it maybe started with a few theories and before she knew it she was onto something really big?"

"Perhaps you have read one too many thrillers or that twit Turner has filled your head with nonsense. There is no escape route; only a few spies doing a little work. People like me who were happy to live quietly, until this." His eyes flared.

"She was just a kid," I shot back at him.

"I admit it was unfortunate, but she is a casualty of war. I must protect myself and the others first. And now there is you Mr. Chapman."

"Yes, there's me and also the authorities here, and in the South, who are very interested in speaking to you."

His eyes flitted to the door for a hair of a second and I rushed him. I swung at his body and at anything around the desk, with pens and books crashing to the floor, my priority was only to unarm him. The gun fell away, he grabbed at me and quickly had my throat. All I could do was butt him with my head. I broke his nose and he let go. He looked French again. He backed away to the door and ran; him seeing that the gun was at my foot. I scooped it up and followed suit. He sailed down the stairs and into the back corridor. I threw myself after him, seconds behind. He was too fast and got through the first two houses, and their dividing doors, well ahead of me. I caught up a little when I got through the third door, padding quietly over the old carpet. I ran for a few more seconds and then paused.

"Stop!" I yelled. He kept running. I gave myself time to aim. I saw the smoke before I heard the shot. He fell to the ground.

I didn't feel good about shooting a man in the back, but, then, he was a murderer and a Nazi. I only winged him, anyway. The police and ambulance came very quickly after my call - it may have been me mentioning the Nazi bit.

***

I spent most of the night at the police station. They get antsy when I solve cases for them. The next day they found Laura buried in Martineau's back garden. He hadn't had the chance to move her yet. Poor girl. The police let me be the one to tell Mrs. Morris the next morning. I felt I owed her that much. I stayed with her during the police interview; it was as if I was her only friend. I had saved her the ransom money, but that didn't mean anything much now.

The sensational headlines died down after a few days and Martineau was shipped off to the mainland, probably to work for the British against the Russians after the war. I never heard anymore about him. I still didn't get around to cleaning my office. I didn't seem to have the stomach for it.

Chapter Twenty-Eight

The police took us both in. He sang like a leprechaun crooning Danny Boy and I wasn't given too hard a time. They were a bit annoyed with me for keeping things to myself but, when it all led to about a dozen arrests here and the same in France, they got over it. I had been on track with most of it and the little boy had indeed been just a picture of some random kid. There were no parents, just lots of criminals. They were even smuggling the cocaine in, in collection boxes and other various merchandise. The white vans with the Sean's Trust logo and the picture on the side did not incur much in the way of security checks it seemed. I returned to my apartment that day with a certain amount of satisfaction. But there was a hollowness to it, too. I was kind of disappointed that the boy was just... nobody. Maybe it was my medication, or maybe it was just a general fatigue with the world and how dark it could be. Perhaps it was the absence of focus or the fear of relapse. I think I was a bit fucking lonely. I allowed myself to think more about my wife, to see if it would be a comfort. It wasn't and I switched off the tap again.

***

About a week later, I was in a Starbucks in town. I had treated myself to a Frappuccino and one of those wee marshmallow things. I was scavenging through my wallet for my loyalty card and happened across what I thought was my PI badge. I absently lifted it out while hunting on. There was no queue and the girl didn't seem to mind. But then I noticed it wasn't my PI licence. I stopped searching and my feet seemed to stick suddenly to the floor. I released an involuntary noise from the back of my throat.

In my hand was a small, plastic, star shaped badge, painted silver. It had SHERIFF etched on it.

Chapter Twenty-Nine

I didn't take much time out to celebrate breaking the case, nor did I really feel like it. I took a few days off though. There had been a card waiting at my house from Mary. It was a best wishes card from after my mother had passed. If I hadn't even found out what I had done in Dublin that would probably been enough to propel me further north again. I left the bombs for trains, again, and was surprised to be greeted by a warm and dry, Antrim evening. I called into the Causeway Hotel and dropped off my bags. I had rung Loach the day before and spoke to him briefly when I arrived. He greeted me warmly and seemed pleased that I had come back. Maggie had already gone to bed but I'm sure she would have given me a radiant welcome. I headed out round to The Nook. No curfew or fear of breaking the strict light and noise regs there. No tee-total agnostic sect to worry 'bout either. I felt like I was fifteen again on holiday in Donaghadee; my first taste of alcohol and tobacco even when that had been some vegetable stewed potteen and a badly made rolly. I have to say, despite the obvious sadness of my last case, I was on a bit of a high along with the sense of anticipation in finishing an older one.

Chapter Thirty

I didn't feel myself for a few days. I had a bit of a runny nose and shrugged it off that I had a touch of flu. I took to my bed and surrounded myself with tissues, Lemsip and cigarettes. I binged on car crash T.V. I like Top Gear. I also had been right not to celebrate that much, anyway. The whole case crumbled over this and that- I'm not sure what exactly, but apparently most of the evidence was only circumstantial and it all unraveled at once. I couldn't believe it. I didn't know what to feel. If I'm honest, I wasn't really feeling myself at all and I didn't know what my next move should be either. But I certainly was gutted. I scrambled to try and make sense of it, to try and put the case back together again. As a last ditch attempt, I contacted an old acquaintance of mine. I usually tried to avoid ex-paramilitaries, though in Northern Ireland it's difficult enough at the best of times. I met him that night in Katy Daly's, in the centre of Belfast.

"What are ya havin'?" he asked.

"Cheers Rab, I'll have a pint of Bass."

We waited at the bar for our drinks, it was around seven and it was just getting over the arrival and departure of students for the six o'clock happy hour. Katy's is a pretty cool alternative bar, often has good music and a friendly atmosphere. It attaches on to The Limelight that a lot of touring rock bands tend to play in. Rab looked like an ageing rocker. He had cropped his receding hair short and still sported a worn out leather jacket. His torso was thin, but his tattooed arms were all muscle.

"Cheers for meeting me, Rab, I appreciate it."

"Not t'all buddy, it's part of ma job these days too."

Hi accent was a strange one. He had the broad, Belfast bit but, from living in Glasgow for a few years, he took some of that with him too. Rab had been a foot soldier, a young buck in the UDA. Our paths had crossed a number of times and more than once I exchanged continued liberty for some information. These days he was a "community worker," but I knew he was still connected. As we chatted, a guy and a girl with acoustic guitars started to play a set, they were good. Unfortunately, they covered some Snow Patrol. No one friggen ever covered Therapy in Belfast anymore. We had another pint, then moved on to shorts.

"So, ya think the lad was in with the paras?"

"Well, that's kind of what I had thought. Or, maybe some rival gang."

"Fuck Brian, I gotta tell ya, it's all fucked up these days. Look at it this way, ya used to have the Prods on one side and the Fens on the other. Aye, it was a bit more complicated, but by and by. Now you've got all fookin' sorts. Bloody Rushkies over here, Poles over there, fuck knows who's working for who."

"Yeah, it's tricky. So, you haven't heard anything about his death."

"Nah Brian, I'm sorry. I'll ask about for ya, but there's been nay said."

"Would you say it was probably connected to drugs?"

"Aye, I suppose, but could just as well of been a couple of wee dopey gangs havin' a spat like. I'll try and find out for ya."

He wasn't filling me with confidence.

"Will we have another drink?" I said.

"Aye, go on."

***

When I woke up the next morning, I felt knackered. I was frigged off too at the way things had panned out. All energy seemed to leave me. I stayed in my flat, unhooked my phone, switched off my mobile. Not many people would miss not hearing from me and I stayed in the flat for three days and spoke to no one. You'd think that the days would drag but when I go like that I don't notice. It's like a curtain comes down, or a bell rings and I know what I must do. It seems to be some kind of self-preservation, maybe. I don't know, I just seem to need it every so often. It's like Dylan says, I just need some "time out of mind."

On the third night, an idea hit me during Top Gear and a half tub of Maud's honeycomb ice cream. I found my car keys, grabbed my smokes and phone and went out to the car. It took a second or two to heat up. I nipped back into the house and grabbed a small, kitchen knife and stuffed it into my jeans. I had also been off my meds for a few days.

It was dark when I parked my car off the Old Park road. I crossed over to Alliance and headed towards the gates to the park on Alliance Parade. I knew this part of North Belfast from my RUC days and knew it to be a favourite spot for coke heads to score. Maybe I'd be able to find something out about the new coke dealers in town. The end of terrace, by the gates, had been derelict for years and had provided shelter to those getting off their face in the park. This used to be a nice street until paramilitaries took over the area and started putting people out. A vulnerable lady with a learning disability had been living in that house quietly until he decided she had to go. He burnt her out. Fortunately, the bastard didn't kill her. I lit up a smoke and pulled the rusty, front gates apart and walked around the back. There was still old material strewn around, more congealed ash than anything else. The stone slabs were still scorched from where the fire brigade had dumped smouldering furniture. At the back step, there were two men in hoodies, smoking. There was a broken washing line lying against the wall beside them and the bathroom window was boarded up with MDF. The grass in the small back garden was at about three foot.

"Alright?" the first man said, casually. They were both about twenty and looked like your average hoods, and this one looked like he could handle himself.

"Dead on," I said, trying to appear like I was on something and not I think very convincingly.

"You looking for someone?" the second asked.

I checked behind me, trying to appear more nervous than I was,

"I'm wanting to score. Can you sort me out?"

They looked at each other, then at me,

"You a nark?" the first asked.

"Of course not," I said, trying to sound incredulous and hard at the same time. "Fuck that."

The first one took a step towards me,

"Maybe we can sort something out, show me your money."

"Alright, cheers," I said, fishing out my wallet and pulling out a twenty and a ten.

"Here's thirty quid," I said, and pushed it into his hand, then took a step back.

They both looked at it and then the second glanced back at the house and towards the low hum of some kind of stoned out gathering taking place. I wasn't sure of their reaction. In fact, I wasn't sure of anything and my confidence began to desert me and I wished I had have stayed in and was watching Emmerdale or something.

"I'm only looking a wee bit," I added, feebly, trying to gauge their reactions.

The first seemed to make up his mind.

"It's okay mate, that'll get you a bag of grass alright," he said, evenly.

I raised an eyebrow and let out an involuntary guffaw. "I'm after a wee bit of coke."

He shook his head and smiled. "No mate, we don't do any heavy shit, just gange."

I started to feel panicked, thinking they were trying to set me up as some kind of mark. Maybe they had friends around the front, blocking any escape.

"Come on" I said, quite breathily. "Give us a few lines."

"Take the grass or fuck off," the second said, impatiently, taking a step closer to stand beside the other.

My mind went blank and I couldn't think straight. The knife was then in my hand and I was moving forward.

"Hey, fuck!" the first spat and both men started walking backwards towards the house.

"Gimme my money back," I wheezed, gesturing with the blade.

"Yo guys! Jimbo, get out here!" the first man shouted towards the rear room of the house.

My head felt woozy and I turned on my heel and sprinted back up the side of the house. The knife felt sweaty in my hand and my brow felt cold and clammy. I felt out of control, but I knew if I concentrated, I could get home in one piece. It's like when you feel so drunk that you can't stand or speak, but you have the clarity to know it will pass.

Chapter Thirty-One

I didn't make it up in time for breakfast. I'm never really sick with drink but I'm sorry to say I had been that night. I didn't quite throw up on a "Wonder of the World," but I did sprinkle a bit on the hotel wall on my way back. I didn't remember getting into bed and I didn't remember singeing the bed sheet with a last cigarette. I must have needed a little blow out. Fortunately, I did remember the conversations I had with the locals and was able to loosen a few tongues enough to find out a little more information on all the key players in my own mystery drama. I took my time washing and getting dressed, and a saint of a chef made me a bacon sandwich even though it was nearly midday. I asked for a phone to rent for my room and I spent half an hour on it to my friend in the home office. He and I go way back to school days. I've done him a few favours over the years and when I need a little information he is nearly always forthcoming. I got the information I needed and felt I was finally getting somewhere. The problem was that some of the information I had been gathering made my stomach sick like after bad rum. I knew I had to keep digging, but things weren't going to be roses and I accepted that. Next, I rang the distillery and pretended to be an importer from Australia. I spoke to Mr. Dufferin's secretary and he would apparently be out the rest of the week. It transpired that he hadn't been away anywhere at all according to her either. I hadn't broken any laws yet, but my accent was criminal. I decided I'd reward myself with some hair of the dog.

Chapter Thirty-Two

When I turned my mobile back on, there were two voicemails. Not much from being off for days. I had got up and washed and decided I needed to leave the house again at some point; whiskey and Coco-pops could only sustain me for so long. After the debacle up at Alliance I had stayed in the house for another two days. The first message was a woman's voice and simply said, "It's me, look I know it's been a while, call me, please." I didn't know who it was, but I felt I should do. It was a soft, Belfast accent with a hint of a middle class background on the vowels. I clicked on to the next message and the same voice spoke, "It's me again. Look, I'm worried about you. Call me."

I sat down at the stool, beside the counter, after pouring a pint of water from the tap. I started to it sink in and tried to make sense of the messages. *Something was nagging me that I knew this voice but why would some woman be so worried about me?* I was momentarily distracted by the state of my small and gloomy kitchen. All of the counters were streaked with grease, coffee granules and splashes of old, curry sauce. The dishes were piled up in the sink and a few cups were a quarter filled with mold. I might have discovered some new miracle medicine growing in there. I refocused, looking out to my small yard; the patch of yellowy grass crowded with dandelions and weeds. It must just be a wrong number, I decided. My phone had been off, so there was no number I could ring back anyway. She sounded anxious, particularly in the second message. I couldn't do anything but see if I heard from her again. Poor girl, whoever she was.

***

It was a better morning, mentally I mean. There are times when you look back at a day earlier, a week, a month and you know that you are in a different place. I suppose we all do that, but I seem to have bigger peaks and troughs than most. I was due to see Mr. Frazer, my psychiatrist at two and thought I should probably go. I'm not deluded enough not to know that sometimes I could do with help. It's better, too, if I keep my appointments and keep the whole multi-disciplinary team off my back. I had a quick lick in the shower, and another coffee, and got out of the house for eleven. The practice is up the Malone Road near the University area. I figured I'd spend the day out and about, take my mind of the case. Maybe I'd hang about in the afternoon and then get to my writer's group in the evening. I parked the Ford off Botanic feeling elated at finding a free space in the busy outskirt of the city centre. I was hungry and treated myself to a burrito at Boojam's. It was friggen delish. The restaurant was full of students, blowing their loans on the pricey wraps and hipster ambience. I'm still not really clear on how to define a hipster exactly, but I'm certain the place was full of them. Anyway, I enjoyed myself and felt fairly relaxed and positive. I headed along Botanic in the direction of Queen's. It's the main hub in the Uni quarter, full of restaurants, bars and some boutique shops. The one I was interested in was for crime fiction buffs. No Alibis is a specialist book shop, the only one of its kind in the country. I took out a few twenties from the cash machine and readied myself to spend a bit of time perusing. The door chimed as I entered and I nodded "Hello" to the owner. He was sitting on a wooden stool at the counter on the left with a coffee and a magazine. I started scouring the shelves for the usual suspects first. I don't know why I always wanted to see what kinds of Chandler, Parker and Stark would be there when I already had all their books. Once I had searched my usual letters I checked out the recommended section. This was back up near the door, opposite the counter and usually had great titles. I wasn't surprised to find several copies of the new Colin Bateman on display. Bateman had set his acclaimed Mystery Man series in none other than the No Alibis shop. The owner saw me looking at it and smiled.

"Yep, that's me," he said.

"Ha ha, I wondered," I said, always happy to have a chat with a bookshop owner. Chatting with a local seller of something that they're passionate about is hard to come by this days. It's not often you find one who has also been fictionalised into a detective series.

"I'm a big Bateman fan," I added. "Mystery man is great. I'm sure you get some random questions from fans."

We went on to have a chat about books and he got me a coffee. *Again, what shops do you get a good chat and a decent coffee too?* The closest would probably be my barber when I pay a tenner for the privilege of some milky instant. I left with three new novels, looking up at the infamous Columbo mural on the ceiling as I left. Just one more thing. As soon as I left the day went pear shaped. The glare of the sunlight struck my eyes after leaving the low-lit store. It's a typical trigger for my migraines. When it comes on, I'm usually primed for one and the way I had been feeling recently made perfect conditions. My sight instantly fell away into a tangle of shapes and colours. I staggered to hold on to a phone box and adjust to the deterioration. What accompanied was also a sudden loss of my good mood and positivity. My thinking clouded with images from the case and dark shapes from the past. I almost buckled and passed out, but I gripped onto the phone box tightly. After thirty seconds or so, if I blinked, I could make out some of my surroundings. I hate it when this happens in public and I must look like a fucking mentalist. Either that or a feckless drunk. I staggered slowly up the footpath, trying to ignore the looks I was sure I'd be getting. Blinking every few seconds to get a sense of where I was, I made it eventually the quarter mile to my car. Pulling myself onto the back seat, relief washed through me. I lay out and pulled my arm over my face to block out the light. It felt good. I didn't give a shit who walked past. I must have lay for about an hour until the vision thing passed and I was just left with the usual, throbbing headache. I sat with my eyes open for a few minutes and the relief was replaced with a general discontentment. I sure as hell wouldn't be going to see my psychiatrist like that. I would ring and say I had flu and get a reschedule. I felt groggy, but was glad I wouldn't have to face the appointment; the relief I felt must have meant I had been dreading it more than I was aware. It felt like that nice part of being sick when you ring into work and know you don't have to go there. I wolfed down a Mars bar and readied myself to drive; that would be the last hurdle.

***

I drove straight home in a daze, I don't remember the journey. I can't remember much about the rest of the afternoon, other than I was determined to make myself be social and go out to my writer's group in the evening. More than that, I'd bring a few chapters along with me too. I had the first proper shower in a long while, shaved thoroughly (not just roughly around my goatee) and even ironed a shirt. I actually got there early and stopped outside when I saw Amy smoking there.

"How you doing?" I said

"Grand, how 'bout you?"

"Not bad," I said, fishing out a smoke and joining her.

"You been signed to any major publishers since I saw you last?" she asked, with a sideward smile, pulling on her cig.

"Just a couple, how 'bout you?"

"No. Well, I did get a new short story published though."

"Oh, very good, where abouts?"

"It's in the new issue of Plan C magazine, it's up on line."

"Dead on, I'll have to check it out."

A few from the class filed past us and we nodded to them. We both stubbed out our cigarettes and went in after them.

"Okay everyone, go. And be kind to each other." Catherwood had told us to split into groups of four and read a paragraph of each other's work and then give feedback to each other. I felt my stomach lurch as we dragged our chairs around to form a group. I was glad I was in a group with Amy, but I hadn't really met the other two. Geraldine was a large, middle aged lady with brown hair and glasses. She was broad and looked like she'd had a pretty, hard life. The other was Kevin, a young guy with short, blonde hair and an affected persona. He seemed the dramatic and know-it-ally type. Great.

"I don't mind," I lied, as we discussed whose work would be read first.

"Okay, great, let's see what you've got," Kevin said. Geraldine changed her glasses and gave me an indifferent look. Neither put me at ease. Amy at least offered me a smile. As they all began to interrogate my prose, I had no notion of what to do with myself. I realised I was staring at them and immediately began to look round the room instead. My heart was beating pretty fast and I felt a thin trickle of sweat on my back. I glanced from table to table and found it was easy to pick out the other writers who had volunteered to go first, too. The seconds dragged and I snuck looks at them to try and read their expressions but couldn't. I stared out the window at the trees lined along University Square, shading the Georgian facades. After a few minutes, Amy stopped reading, glanced at me and smiled. The other two stopped soon after, but I couldn't read their expressions. There was an awkward silence.

"I'll go first," Amy said. "I really enjoyed it, it's well written, Brian. I like the Billy Chapman character."

"Thanks," I said, nodding nervously. "Anything you didn't like?" I ventured.

"Well, I... maybe wasn't sure about some of the historical accuracy?" she said, awkwardly.

"Like what?" I asked, and it was out of my mouth and a little sharper than I had meant.

"Well, she said...."

"There's a few things" Kevin chimed in, feigning an aversion to picking faults in others. "For example, Dublin didn't have a huge air raid like you describe."

"They actually did Kevin," I said, trying to stay composed.

"I am just after completing my HND and I'm afraid you're mistaken. It did not happen in that way, there were just a couple of small bombs off target."

I noticed Catherwood glancing over, aware of the faintly raised voices.

"I've read a lot of books on this, and visited a lot of museums and libraries, it definitely did and on the date I describe," I said, trying to end the argument, going for a knockout, not wanting ten rounds. Kevin looked indignant but, before he could respond, Amy interrupted.

"I liked the style, I really did," she said, with an anxious smile. I think we all had forgotten about Geraldine until she removed her glasses.

"I'm sorry, I didn't like it. I think it was a wee bit rubbish. Sorry Brian," Geraldine said.

It made me give up the battle,

"Thanks for all your comments, who's next?" I said, trying not to appear crushed and regretting ever showing anyone anything.

I managed to stay and seethe through the next turn, so not to appear completely obvious when I left. It was Kevin's, who all seemed to enjoy his paragraphs. I made my clumsy excuses about how I really had to go before offering any feedback. Amy looked sorry for me and I fumbled a quick excuse to Catherwood on my way out. He looked puzzled. As I made my way down the corridor, I felt a weird mix of elation for getting out of there and frustration at all the other aspects. I had a smoke in my hand ready by the time I exited the building and was heading down University Street. My head was awash again with the case, my story and my past.

I was so pissed off when I got home. I was pissed at myself for losing it and for realising I wasn't out of my rut yet either. I was pissed, too, cause I downed half a bottle of Jack Daniels. The cycle continued and I went back to bed for a couple of days, I'm not sure how many.

Chapter Thirty-Three

I made the short walk to the Causeway School around three o'clock. It sits on a hill about a ten minute walk from the hotel. It is a wonderful building designed by Clough Williams Ellis famous for creating the fairytale village Portmeirion in Wales. The school is an appropriate addition to the ethereal quality of this community, sitting proudly in the shadow of the Causeway. There was something of Kantian Park here, too. There was also a slight coldness but I preferred that to the somewhat artificial nature of Kantian Park. I had visited Portmeirion some ten years earlier. It is an incredible collection of buildings, creating a dream like village. It had had a similar quality, but it only contained the good aspects. I had been eager to see Mary as soon as I saw her leave the bar that April night. After that phone call with my contact, my eagerness had been superseded by resigned dread. As I walked up the steps, the door opened and about twenty kids started to file out of the door quietly. I could see Mary at the end of the room collecting up some papers. She had a presence with the children. I could see it. I wish I had had a teacher who looked like that... no I don't... I would have got even worse grades.

"Billy," she said, affectionately, walking up the aisle of the room. "I'm so pleased you came back."

"Hello Mary, I hope this isn't a bad time."

"No, you're grand, it's so nice to see you," she said, sweetly. "Would you like a wee cup of tea?"

"That'd be great, please. Is there somewhere we can talk privately?"

Her smile strained a little.

"Yes, of course, we'll go into my office."

She had a small room at the back of the main school room with a desk and a couple of chairs and a bookcase, but little else. I felt like I was meeting an old girlfriend from junior school. I had to remind myself that I didn't even really know her.

"What can I do for you, did you get my card?" she asked, sipping her tea.

"Yes, I did, yes, thank you." I couldn't bear any small talk. "I suppose I'll come straight to the point."

I switched the crossing of my legs and set my cup down. I don't like tea anyway.

"Mary, I don't want to upset you and I don't want to be indelicate. The thing is I do want to get to the bottom of this thing and there's no getting away from it."

As much as anyone actually can, I think she turned a little green. She set down her cup too and mimicked my crossed legs, but didn't utter a word.

"Okay, so it's like this. I don't think you met a serviceman and went to England to marry him. You'll have to forgive me, but I've done some digging. That particular regiment was never stationed where you said and there is no marriage licence recorded for you anywhere."

I felt bad, but there was nothing else for it. She continued to look at me with a vague expression of not quite anger nor pain.

"I think you had a relationship with Frank and you became pregnant. I think you had to leave because this community would never accept a baby out of wedlock, never mind one between cousins."

I was suddenly panicked in case I had been wrong.

"Second cousins," she said quietly, speaking for the first time. Her eyes had welled up and she dabbed at them briefly with a pale linen handkerchief. "Why are you saying all this? If it's true what does it matter anyway now?" She stopped and then asked, urgently, "Have you told anyone any of this?"

"No, of course not, and I won't," I replied, definitely.

I lit both of us a cigarette and passed her one. She inhaled deeply and looked beyond me for a few, lingering seconds. She then composed herself and looked at me softly in the face.

"Hardly anyone ever knew. I loved him very much." She leaned to the side and propped her arm on her knee, "What do you want to know?"

"I really am sorry to be bringing all of this up with you. The reason is that I think someone knew about you two and was blackmailing Frank. Have you any idea who would do something like that?"

"Blackmail? No, he didn't have any enemies. Frank didn't have much money either. I don't know what someone would do that for."

"Neither do I, but I intend to find out. Do you know why Frank left the distillery all that time ago? Was it anything to do with the baby?"

"No, I don't think so. I mean, he was revaluating things I suppose when I went away but, no, not really. Wait," she said, slowly. "There was something, I think. Yes, there was an altercation with someone one night in The Nook."

"Do you know what it was about?"

"I'm sorry, I've no idea. I do remember Frank was very worked up around that time actually, but I mostly put it down to me being, well, pregnant. It wasn't that long after I left right enough that he told me how he was going to leave the Distillery."

"Do you remember who the fight was with?"

She thought hard for a few seconds.

"I think maybe John something, John Fitzgerald maybe?"

"Ferguson?"

"Yes, Ferguson."

Chapter Thirty-Four

The sunlight and fresh air were a jolt to my system and I pulled my hoody tightly around me. I was exposed from my cocoon of stale smoke and artificial light. My only desire had been to stock up on cigs and snacks, but when I emerged into the outside world I almost had a full blown panic attack. I had been avoiding thinking about the case going wrong and I had let my last prescription run out too. I got a call from the police that morning, too. They had said that there was actually no case at all now and I could not go within spitting distance of Cantrell for six months. It was fucking unbelievable. It was making me crazy. I got my smokes and decided I'd get the munch later. I walked back to my flat and grabbed my car keys, then hopped in the car.

"Brian, you look like a fucking dog's dinner," Jemma said, when she ushered me into the little studio. We had to squeeze past a few people in the corridor and she actually looked a bit embarrassed.

"I know, I've had a rough few days. Bit of flu and that," I lied. "This bloody case has been doing my head in too."

We sat down together and had a coffee each again, but there was no jovial atmosphere like the time before. There was something different in her face.

"Brian, do you need... do you need a bit of help?"

"No, I'm fine, but I could do with some more of your professional input."

"Look, the guy Greg called me yesterday. He told me he had been doing some digging for you. Fuck, Brian, you shouldn't have asked him to do that."

"He wanted to Jem, he just said he would talk to a few mates. I said I'd pay him for it."

She shook her head and her hair hung to the side. Her face looked anxious,

"Brian, he's scared, he's away down South to stay with friends for a few weeks. I think he's asked too many questions and he's freaked himself out."

"Well, there you are then, no harm done," I said. I sat forward and clasped my hands together, "Right. I was hoping that you would write and publish the first part of the story."

"I don't understand? What story? All there is, is unsubstantiated talk about a kid running some drugs. I'm not even working for a paper at the minute."

"I know Jen, but you have your contacts. Look, I'm so close to cracking it all. There's a link too with a charity, I know it sounds crazy, but there is. They've been bringing in coke...."

"Wow, hold on," she interrupted. "Have you proof of any of this?"

"Not exactly, but...."

"Frig me Brian, what's happened to your filter? Even if I had some contacts interested, how could I print a story with no substantiation and no one on record?"

I stopped for a second and tried another tack.

"Come on Jen, you're still a hungry journalist, you wouldn't want to miss out on a huge story."

She looked pained and I suppose plain worried.

"I'm sorry Brian, I can't."

***

After controlling myself sufficiently to enter the local Spar for some junk to munch on, I decided on three things, albeit half-heartedly. One, I would crack this case for good, two, I would take a break from my meds and three, I would finish my story. Oh, I also decided to go on a wee trip to Ards.

Chapter Thirty-Five

I made myself stay away from the shorts all afternoon to keep a clear head. I was planning on going to a distillery, by myself, after hours so that was dangerous enough for a start. It was all but pitch dark at eight o'clock, but I had brought a torch and a few tools. After trying to look casual sauntering through Bushmills village, I quickly climbed over the outside fence. There were no security men working at night. I suppose there didn't need to be because the actual distillery, and the safe room, were fairly impenetrable. I only wanted to get into a few offices, in a separate building, and was relying on them not being too secure. I crossed carefully through the courtyard and up the side of the main production area. I found the office block around the side with a few trees, to the side, looking as if they were leaning in to listen. The offices looked quite different from the outside but I had a rough idea of how to get back to Colrain's one. I walked along both sides and tried all of the ground floor windows, but had no luck. The first floor looked a bit ropey to try and get up to, so I went for Plan B. I found a decent-sized window that opened to the side near to where I hoped Colrain's office was. I put a tea towel over the glass and frame and knocked gently, twice, with the small hammer I had liberated from behind Maggie's desk. It cracked quietly. I repositioned the towel and knocked through a few inches of glass. That made a little more noise as it fell inwards. I reached around carefully, and opened up the latch. I then sat down on the grass beneath the window and waited for five minutes to make sure no one had heard. I crept inside, cautiously. I was just a few offices away from Colrain's and had a cursory look through each one as I went. I didn't see anything very interesting, but hadn't expected to. I soon found Colrain's office next door to Ferguson's smaller one. I only knew that because it had an ostentatious sign with his name on it that he must have thought was tasteful. I searched both rooms and found little of any use that is probably because I was playing a hunch and didn't really know what I was looking for. I made a big show of tidying up enough to make it clear someone had been there searching. It took me longer to find Mr. Dufferin's office. It was on the first floor and was through a small receptionist's room. It was a nice room, much more my style if I could have afforded to have any. I didn't do any searching there, just took a piece of his headed paper and wrote him a letter, put it in an envelope and set it neatly on his desk. I waited until I was safely on the road again through the village before my sweaty hands lit up a smoke.

Chapter Thirty-Six

I admit that I'm not sure how I ended up going to Ards. Ards is a shithole. It really is. It's five miles up the road from Bangor. At least they know they're in a shithole. I had gotten the bus from the Upper Newtownards Road and traveled through Dundonald and up the carriageway to Ards. Before that, I drove over to Lisburn to see Tim. I decided that I'd talk the case through with him and see if that got me anywhere either with the case or with my growing obsession with it. I had started to feel like both the case and my story were starting to drag me down. I was entwined with both and wanted to see them through. I suppose it's like most things, when it's not fun anymore but you're invested in it, it becomes a chain. I was dragging around too many chains. As I approached the house I found that an ambulance was parked outside, sirens and lights off. The old door, with scratched green paint, showing some old yellow underneath lay open. For some reason, I was suddenly aware of my scruffiness and ran a hand through my hair and did up my jacket buttons.

"Hello?" I said, lightly knocking the glass panel as I then started down the hall.

"Yes, in here," a voice said, that wasn't Tim's. The body joined the voice and came out into the hall, a male paramedic dressed in green.

"Is Tim okay," I asked. "I was coming to visit him."

"Come on through," he answered, reassuringly and led me through to the living room. The doorway was momentarily blocked by a young, female paramedic bending over to retrieve something from a large medicine bag.

"Hello," she said. I smiled, but was anxious to see past her. I went on through and there was Tim.

"You pick your moments," he said, trying to sound casual. Tim was on the floor, propped up awkwardly against the bottom of his favourite chair. It looked as though the other two weren't long arrived and had just helped to sit him up.

"Are you okay?" I asked weakly, not knowing where to stand or what to do with my hands.

"I'll be okay," he said, appearing in some pain and embarrassment. "Just had a wee fall."

"Excuse us," the man said, coming past with a stretcher, the girl bringing over a stethoscope.

"Look, I'm in the way here. Is there anything I can do?" I asked, longing for someone to give me a reprieve to get out of there.

The two paramedics carried on working around Tim.

"No, no I'm going up for a checkup now, but I'll be fine," Tim said, with waning bluster. He looked weak, crumpled.

"Well, take care okay? I'll check in with the hospital later... and see you soon."

I almost ran from the house. I went home, left off my car and grabbed my bag. My head was already up my arse. I tried to put it out of my mind as the bus trundled along, stop by stop. I checked into a small bread and breakfast in the town centre. Once I got to Ards I just felt fucking depressed anyway and it wasn't the dream, but I was happy that I had my objectives and treated myself to a little daytrip. I looked round the town and it wasn't quite as bad as I had remembered. The Town Hall market area is alright and they had a Nero on the corner, so I got a decent coffee at least. I was disappointed despite my low expectations that there wasn't more in the town. There wasn't one record shop or book shop. *What did people do in Ards?* Well, they seemed to drink if the number of off sales and ruddy noses were anything to go by. I did ring the hospital after a few hours. Tim had been admitted, but nothing was broken and it was just for observation. I asked them to pass on my best and it made me feel a bit better for my total uselessness earlier. I decided to make the most of my adventure to the depth of Down. I couldn't remember the last time I had gone anywhere as a tourist. Maybe I was trying to do something vaguely normal for a change. Everyone needs a holiday, right? Northern Ireland is apparently a hot draw these days with the likes of Game of Thrones and that; though, anyone looking for hot beaches and hot girls will be sorely disappointed. They'd have better luck finding dragons.

Chapter Thirty-Seven

I slept well that night and only had a few shorts before bed. I had a quiet morning, followed by a quiet lunch time and early afternoon. I also felt a continuous sense of anticipation and, I suppose, excitement. I stayed around the hotel the whole day so it would be easy for someone if they wanted to ring or come and speak to me. Nobody did. I didn't even see Mr. Loach and Maggie was even less chatty than usual. There was one assault on my positive mood though. I was listening to the wireless and Bing Crosby's crooning was interrupted by a breaking news report. The afternoon news saddened me and, after not long leaving Dublin, I felt a keen sense of loss. Maybe it was because of what I knew could happen to a city, like it had in Belfast. The mark of war hung in Belfast for a long time, like the manure and grit that had been put on to camouflage the Stormont Parliament; it took years to fade. It still has a remnant on the bricks today. Dublin had suffered its worst bombing campaign and ninety souls, at least, had been killed outright. The city was in shock and in widespread confusion. I wondered if anyone at Kantian Park would even have noticed the raid. I was damn sorry for all of them. I had a couple of pints over the day and read a couple of day old papers, trying to remain upbeat. I got over the nasty feeling and went back to the general resignation that I think most people felt in those days. I had a nice cup of coffee and a piece of buttery shortbread about three in the afternoon. I was happy that things seemed to be going to plan up here at least; so about four I rang Ferguson. It took a little time and bluffing to get him on the other end of the line, but when I did it was worth it. I told him how I knew everything (though I didn't) and gave him just enough of what I did know to reel him in.

"If you've been into my office you're going to be in a lot of trouble Chapman," he had said, in his hoarse Antrim growl.

"Well, maybe one of us will be in a lot of trouble," I replied. "Let's meet up for a nice chat about it."

I said I wanted to meet him at eight o'clock on the other side of the Causeway stones, through the tunnel and looking out towards the Giant's pipe organ. He was curt and said he didn't know what rubbish I was talking, but he'd be there just the same. I was fairly reassured that he and Dufferin hadn't spoken about anything yet. I came off the phone pleased with myself. I headed straight for an early dinner because my stomach was churning with something or other.

Chapter Thirty-Eight

Ards town wasn't going to peak my interest for long and keep my mind off of things. The B&B was a novelty though. It wasn't anything fancy, but it was homely. It was nice to be in a different room, too, in a different place. There's something about the starched sheets; bought more for durability than comfort, and having a mini kettle with a bowl of coffee and milk sachets beside. I got the bus to both the outskirts and to Scrabo Tower Country Park. I got off at the upper car park, at the foot of the steep climb to the folly. Scrabo was designed like a fairy tale turret and the Londonderrys built it as a monument to the family. I'd visit their country home afterwards. I set off at a quick pace and avoided smoking on the climb. There weren't many about and the wind whistled across the face of the hill, running off the adjoining, golf course green. At the summit, it's always a surprise how large the tower actually is. It makes sense when it stands tall and lean and can be viewed from all sides of Strangford Lough. I walked out to the edge of the rock face and had a smoke. My mind glazed over for a while and I drifted. *What would it be like to fall from here or to jump? Would I cry out?* My focus returned slowly to my eyes looking out over Ards. What a hole.

I went on to my next jolly. Mount Stewart sits along the Ards Peninsula, on the edge of Strangford Lough. It is a stately home and gardens now, run by the National Trust, formerly the home of the Marquee of Londonderry. The bus left me off at the turquoise gates and I paused to glance at the glistening Lough, with Scrabo Tower framed to my right in between mature oaks and palm trees. Mount Stewart has its own micro-climate that offers a continental flavour to the many gardens and forests. The

Londonderry's were a well-traveled family as well and this virtue was reflected in the Chinese gardens and within the house with many ornaments and artifacts from round the world. I paid my seven fifty at the desk and considered asking them to wear a mask the next time. I took the free map and set off for a walk around the lake. It was a fantastic day with a low sun and cool breeze, the gardens protected bin part by the surrounding forests. There were few visitors with it being mid-week and out of season. My feet seemed to make a loud trampling sound on the loose stones as I crossed in front of the house and towards the formal gardens. I had been on somewhat of an autopilot and started to reflect on what I was doing. An old man with a walking stick walked past me and I nodded a greeting. He nodded back, stiffly. Maybe I didn't look like the average National Trust enthusiast. 'What are you doing?' I asked, myself. 'What? I'm just having a little day trip. You know what I mean.'

I suppose I hadn't been honest with myself and, perhaps, I was running away a little bit. I didn't know how things were going to go with the case and, maybe, I just wasn't coping all that well generally. I circled the pond in around half an hour at a leisurely pace. I felt some peace that had been missing from my average day. I headed towards the Chinese gardens as a small, two man plane flew overhead. There is a little airstrip nearby that used to be owned by the family. They were friendly with prominent Nazis prior to the last war and even flew over to visit the Gorings. Perhaps this could find its way into my story. I felt a pang that I needed to get back to working on it. I suppose it had already become a bit of an obsession. It had become something I do like drink or smoke. It had worked its way into part of my ordinary fabric. Well, my psychiatrist always said, "Maintain your mental health daily," and writing was now playing a big part of that. I walked on, smiling at this realisation that, for whatever it was worth, I could call myself 'A Writer.' The formal gardens were impressive and kept like a pin. They were grander than I remembered; it had probably been ten years since I had last seen them. I leaned against the old, stone wall and took in the ponds, hedges and follies. I let my mind drift in and out of the case. I still hadn't heard anything back from Eric so I took out my phone and called him. I let it ring off twice and on the third try he answered.

"Brian?"

"Yeah, it's me, how you doing Eric?"

"Spotty dog," he answered, slowly. "Are you okay though?"

"Yeah, why do you ask? Look, have you found anything out yet?"

There was a pause. He sounded distracted.

"No mate, I'm sorry. Look, I think you just should leave it, maybe. Do you not think you should leave it? You've been saying some strange things."

"No, where's this coming from?"

"I'm sorry Bri, gotta go, my battery's gonna die."

He hung up. I couldn't understand what his problem was. Total melt, and a fucking, let down. I went for coffee and a slice of Victoria sponge in the café to chill out. The free WiFi allowed me to do a bit more Googling on the case and a little bit for my story, too. I found out little else for the case, but came across a few WWII sites that I hadn't seen before. I started to wonder again how the story should end. *Maybe I should kill Billy off?* That would be a shame, though, particularly if I wanted to write a sequel. 'Catch yourself on you goat,' I said, to myself. I stayed for two hours in the little café and had it all but to myself. I made a phone call to the hospital to see how Tim was doing.

"Yes, Mr. Cairns has actually been discharged."

"Has he gone home, how is he doing?"

"You said you were not family, so I am afraid I cannot give you out that information."

"Look he doesn't have any family and I'm worried about him. Just tell me if he's gone home... please."

There was a pause.

"I cannot tell you where Mr. Cairns has gone, but I am afraid he will now require nursing care."

I lapped around the lake again and thought about Tim. Poor guy. I'd have to find out where he had gone and go and see him. Maybe he'd need me to help clear out his house. Jesus, maybe if he died, he'd need me to oversee his wishes. I was angry at myself for thinking like that. I was angry at myself for dwelling on things too, when there's Eric, shipped off to a home.

By the time I walked up to the bus stop to take me back to Ards, I had decided what I would do next. I would visit the Causeway and would stay until I had either finished my story or completed my case. I can see now that I was smack in the middle of a high-functioning psychosis.

Chapter Thirty-Nine

After a few libations, I walked down to the Causeway a little before it got dark. I left about six so that I could be fairly sure I would be there first. The wind blew me along the downward path in between the cliffs, but it was dry and my insides were warm with whiskey and meat. The moon lit up the hexagonal rocks stretching out to sea and Scotland as the sun when down. On a night like this the myth didn't seem quite as fanciful. Once I got to the passageway, I pulled out my glistening palms and reached into my jacket fishing out a cigarette and lighter. I then watched and smoked, smoked and watched, for the next hour.

Chapter Forty

I felt uneasy as I asked for my single ticket to Bushmills. I had picked up the bus from Ards the next morning, to Belfast Central, arriving there at around eleven. I had time to ring the Causeway Hotel to book a room before needing to catch my connecting bus to head up the M2. The large hallway beneath the train station contained a few, straggling, school children, but was mostly full of innocuous men and women going about their daily commute. I stepped out of the hall and, all of a sudden, I felt very unwell and flailed about to rest down on a plastic bench. A few travelers inched further away from me. I probably looked like an old wino. The seat felt like ice and a trickle of sweat slid down beneath my shirt. I clung to the seat with both hands and felt consciousness leaving me. I was fairly used to this kind of thing by then. It didn't leave me altogether and instead a ringing began in my ears and a warmth returned and soared through my body. I rubbed my clammy hands on my blue jeans clinging to my thighs. It passed. A few minutes later and the bus arrived and I was fortunate to get a window seat and a free seat for my bag. As the bus journeyed through the bustle of the early evening dusk, I felt something strange. An excitement and, also, incredible apprehension. I recalled school trips to the zoo, the farm, even one to The Causeway. There was no smell here of cheese sandwiches though and Tayto cheese and onion. As we passed The Waterfront Hall, then City Hall, then The Grand Opera House, my mind drifted to The Causeway. *Would it be how I had remembered it and tried to translate it into my story? Would I find inspiration to crack the Teenage Wristband case for good? Would I have enough cigarettes I thought urgently? I'd have to stop off at a Centra.*

Chapter Forty-One

I made Ferguson out when he was about halfway down the slope. The moon bounced off his jacket buttons and his cigarette end danced like a firefly. I stood openly in the middle of the tunnel with my hands out, smoking. We watched each other as the distance between us shortened. When he was a few paces away, I couldn't even hear his footsteps as the waves lapped beside us. The faint smell of drying seaweed was pleasant on the air.

I padded back through the tunnel to the far side and he followed me. We didn't say anything. I turned to face him as we came out the other side. I threw my cigarette to the ground and he did the same.

Chapter Forty-Two

As soon as I came past the signs welcoming me to Bushmills, I felt incredibly sick. The bus was stuffy anyway. I had also woken abruptly after dozing off and then having a disturbing dream. My wife was swimming around me in a pool and kept diving under. I strained to look at her, but couldn't see her face. Thank God I didn't wake myself up with a scram this time. There was significant humidity on the bus and I had been cooped up for a couple of hours. I dragged myself off and waited my turn to grab my holdall from underneath the chassis. The bus drove away, visitors wandered off and I stood alone in the car park with my things, not sure what to do. I didn't even fancy a smoke. Eventually, I padded over to a row of benches and sat down. I looked across the car park and could see the Bushmills Hotel looking smart and expensive. Every few minutes, small groups of tourists filed past and a bus would enter the car park and leave again. The Causeway Hotel was only a five minute taxi journey away, but something was stopping me from going there. I felt like a child who had got lost on holiday and didn't know where to go. I hope that wasn't what I looked like. I used to be in the police for fuck sake. I knew I wasn't feeling right, but I just went with it. I was bloody sick of being so up and down. I just wanted it to end. I queued up at the third bus lane and waited. I didn't know where it went to. Five minutes later a Goldliner arrived and I got on.

I sank back into the garish, striped seat and tried to get comfy. I put my bag on the seat beside me and stared out the window. I allowed my pulse to slow and tried some breathing exercises. Maybe I should have kept up taking my meds. The bus was around half full and contained mostly retired Americans in highly flammable, shell suits. I checked that I had my lighter. The bus sped through the town, just stopping once and then took off in the direction of the Causeway. It stopped near The Nook, down from the visitor centre. I looked away and out towards the hills, a patchwork of farms of green and yellow. There was a lot of bustle and the quite pleasant noise of suitcases being wheeled over gravel. I didn't look up towards the hotel and instead closed my eyes and tried to make my mind go blank. It didn't of course and instead it started to meander through the case; the dead teen, Sean, cocaine, the botched arrests. I needed some time to sit down and write everything out and try to work this case out. I needed to end it. It was a while before I realised we had set off again and I opened my eyes in time to see we were passing the old, school house. I felt sleepy, I closed my eyes and drifted off.

I looked at my watch, it was almost two in the afternoon. I felt quite hungry. I stifled a yawn and looked out the thinly, misted window. We were just passing Dunluce Castle; the ancient ruins precariously hanging on the edge of the Antrim cliffs. The next dropping off point was Carrick-a-rede and the famous rope bridge. I found myself grabbing my things and then making my way off the bus. Some others did the same and, after a few minutes, the big wheels spun and the coach went off to climb some more of the cliffs. It would reach Torr Head next and would need every inch of tread in those tyres. I was standing on the edge of a large, gravel, car park quite full with six of seven coaches at the far end. I had never visited there before and I could make out a small, visitor centre and toilets before a kiosk and what I presumed was the start of the walk to the bridge.

"Five sixty, please."

"How much? To walk across a bridge?" I asked, attempting to sound good humoured.

"Yes sir," the polite and humourless student answered.

"Okay, the National Trust is doing well out of me this week. Just as well, I'm a Unionist."

She didn't give any reaction, just continued to smile faintly. I gave her six quid and when she passed my change, I went to put it in the charity box. I froze. I recognised that logo, the colours. I dropped the money in and it seemed to take a long while to chink in with the rest of the coins.

"Here's your map sir," the girl said, and diligently started to explain the route and points of interest. I didn't really listen, but stared at her face as she spoke.

"You guys know about Sean's Trust up here too then," I broke in.

"I'm sorry?"

"The collection jar," I gestured with my hand, Sean's Trust."

She looked at it puzzled and then back at me.

"That's Amnesty International Sir."

I spun the jar round and inspected it. She was right.

"Sorry, I was mistaken."

***

The first step was the worst. Or maybe even the couple of steps down to the beginning of the bridge. That's where you can really see how high you are. A Japanese couple had just stepped off when I got on. There was a queue of tourists behind me, too, which gave me a feeling of claustrophobia. Just as well I don't really have a fear of heights, too. As I walked, I zipped up my jacket, the wind cut through the sunshine between these two big lumps of rock. I stared straight ahead for the first half and as I felt more confident, I glanced down as I walked. It took my breath, like a twenty deck of reds. Waves crashed below and gulls were even flying underneath me. It was dramatic and it made me feel alive. When I reached the island, I found a mossy clump of rock and sat down and ate a sandwich I had bought from the visitor centre. I lit up a smoke. I felt peaceful for a few minutes. My mind wasn't racing to try and make me concentrate on or solve something for a while. It was quiet. If I had known what the rest of the day would bring, I would have stayed there.

I stared up at the mustard coloured ceiling, all the more jarring against newly coated, royal blue walls. I let myself float in whatever direction the water took me. I hadn't lay on my back in a pool for years. I had ended up spending the afternoon in the bar of the Lunny Hotel in Coleraine. It had seen better days, but I doubted the so called spa had ever seen average days. Something possessed me to buy some trunks and convince the manager to let me pay to use the leisure facilities. The few residents staying there had all thought better than to try it and I enjoyed the solitude. The gentle lapping eased my mind and allowed it to open up a little bit. I could feel some pain seep in and I knew somehow that I should. When changed and refreshed in the musty, worn changing area, I knew it was time to take one last trip.

***

I arrived at The Causeway Hotel in the late part of the evening, drenched. I felt ready and keen now. The heaven's had opened just after the bus dropped me outside the new visitor centre. It is a finely designed construction, rising like a giant piece of cake at a slope to the side of the cliff. The roof is blanketed in grass and from above appears to be a natural hill. A few minutes was enough to launder my clothes while still on me. I paused a few feet from the oddly curved building of the hotel, to take it in and it was just as I had remembered it. The weather was the same, too. I shook myself off in the porch and entered the main hall; a new coat of grey covered the old walls and fresh gloss had touched up the cornicing. There was no one on reception and the hall was quiet with a few residents and waiters carousing between the bar and the formal dining room. I walked up to the desk and pressed my hand lightly on the service bell. A familiar face stepped out from the back office. It was Maggie.

I tried to control my breathing in the hot shower that engulfed it and keep my mind from disintegrating into mush.

'You're just having a small hallucination, it's okay. You'll be fine, it'll pass."

"It's not okay," I shouted back at myself. She's a character in my fucking story!"

I longed for my medication and I pined for some whiskey, but I was determined to have neither. I know my face had whitened when I saw hers and God knows what I said to whoever that was on reception. I could feel colour returning and I was safe in my warm, double room. Maybe she was just some woman who looked a bit like Maggie. Fuck- it was only in my imagination in the first place. I don't remember how I got back to my room. I'd be secure with my clean linen, trouser press and TV with three working channels. "It's okay, it'll pass," I thought.

***

I got dressed into clean clothes, shaved, put on deodorant and did all the usual things someone does to focus the mind and calm the fuck down. I plugged in the mini kettle and made myself a complimentary, instant coffee and had a piece of Walkers shortbread. For some strange reason, I switched my mobile back on and checked for any messages. I suppose I was self-regulating. There was one, but this time I recognised the nasal drone.

"Brian, this is Nicola from the social work team, I've been trying to reach you. Look, could you give me call please on 0783568472. Brian," she paused. "I'm worried about you, we're worried about you. Myself and Amanda, your community nurse would really like to see you," she paused again and grew harder. "We need assurances Brian, okay, call me please."

'Fuck that,' I said, out loud and turned the phone back off again. I took a breath, lit a cigarette and then set my laptop up on the writing desk.

I worked in a frenzy. The words danced in front of me. I lost myself in a haze of fiction.

Chapter Forty-Three

"So, what's all this about?"

"I wanted somewhere for us to talk where we could be alone," I said.

"So talk."

"I know everything, Ferguson."

"I'm sure you do and what is that, exactly?"

"You killed Frank McKenzie up there on that cliff," I said, pointing up above. We both looked up for a second.

"Did I? And why would I do that?"

He shuffled a little where he stood.

"You were blackmailing him and he had had enough of it."

He stopped shuffling for a second.

"Blackmail?" he scoffed, and made a face. "I don't know what you're talking about. You know nothing."

"I know he had a baby with his cousin."

That made him pay attention. He licked his lips and, unconsciously, he moved closer to me.

"I know that he must have told you when you worked together at the distillery. I know that you had a fight about it. Though there was more than just that."

I left that hanging.

"Go on," he said, urgently. "What other nonsense have you got?"

I lit a cigarette slowly and blew some smoke towards the sea.

"The other reason he left was because you wanted him to start a little scam with you, but he wouldn't do it. I did some digging and I know that you have built up quite the skim up at the distillery. You'd been stealing cases and selling them on the black market, but the demand was

getting too much and it was harder to keep it going. It was getting harder to cover your paper trail at the distillery too. So, you called on Frank to use his boat to help you; maybe to take them to Rathlin Island or somewhere before they would get picked up. Things had got a bit more difficult with the war on. He didn't want any part of it but you said you would expose him if he didn't. But he didn't do it for himself, he did it for Mary."

Ferguson had a quick glance all around him and appeared to be thinking very hard. He lit up a smoke and spoke in a quiet, cold voice.

"You can't prove anything, Chapman. You're got nothing on me. You've got a whole lot of, I don't know, ideas just."

"I got plenty. There's enough to get you sent down. You killed a man."

"I didn't kill him!" he shouted, suddenly before lowering his voice again. "He fell." He looked at me straight, took a draw and threw his cigarette down. "So, you're right. It doesn't matter anyway, but not about that. He tried to fight me. I don't know. He went crazy. We fought and he fell. I didn't mean for it to happen."

"Well, that makes it okay then."

"I really don't care what you think 'bout anything. But, yeah, you were pretty close on most things."

He pulled out a forty five and aimed it around my chest.

"It's unregistered. No trace."

"Is it?" I said, trying to sound disinterested.

"You haven't been talking to anyone else now have you?" he asked, stepping up beside me and patting me down.

"I could say I was just off the phone with Orson Welles and he's going to make a film about you, but what's the point?"

He licked his lips again and looked around.

"Go stand over there," he commanded, gesturing to the foot of the cliff, his voice faltering a little. I did as I was told and tried to stay composed.

"One thing I should mention is that your boss, Mr. Dufferin is standing on the other side of that tunnel and has just heard everything you've said."

He looked startled, then confused then angry all in around one and a half seconds. "What are you talking about now?"

"Like I said."

"You're talking out of your hat."

"Okay, maybe I am. Truth is I don't know for sure, but does that not worry you a little bit?"

He looked towards the tunnel and then at me and held the gun looser and to the side. He gestured for me to go on towards it.

"I wrote him a letter you see, left it on his desk, just after I made a show of checking the offices. I told him everything and in particular to come down here for eight and stand round that side of the rock and listen to you spilling your guts."

"Shut your mouth, gumshoe."

"Go on and take a look if you don't believe me."

He chewed on it for a second.

"Right, go on through then and stay close," he said, sapping me once to the small of my back. It stung a little, but I tried not to flinch. I also tried to think what the heck I'd do if no one was on the other side of this pile of stones. We idled back through and the sound of the waves melded with the wind running through echoing all around us. As I came through, I couldn't see anyone. I pretended to trip and then feinted to the side. I spun around with my elbow in his face as hard as I could. His nose sprayed blood over the rocks and he lifted the gun towards me. I punched his wrist and the gun fell somewhere. He grabbed me around the neck and we rolled along the ground and out of the tunnel.

"Hold it!" a voice said. The voice was calm and authoritative. We both stopped still on good extinct and looked up. We were looking down the barrel of a shotgun; one barrel each. The man was crouched on the bottom of the rocks and stood up slowly. He was nearly sixty, bearded, thin and dressed in an expensive green suit.

Ferguson was next to stand. "Look Mr. Dufferin, I...."

"Quiet," Dufferin said, softly but firm. "Please get up won't you, Mr. Chapman."

I got up last and dusted myself off a little.

"I'm pleased you came. I'm glad you could read my writing."

"Quite. You and I have things to discuss."

Suddenly, Ferguson threw a handful of gravel into Dufferin's face. Dufferin stumbled slightly, dropped his gun and clawed his hands at his eyes. I moved to grab Ferguson, but he was already sprinting towards the sheer cliff face to the left of us. I pursued and he was already climbing. He was making good progress even with next to nothing to hold onto. I started to climb up behind, but was nowhere close to him. I got a few meters up and thought better of it. I had been through enough not to throw it all away with a dive off of the Causeway. I carefully made my way back down, Ferguson still rapidly heading in the other direction. Dufferin and I stared up the cliff face together and waited for the inevitable. Ferguson was about three quarters of the way almost when we heard him shout. I could just make out his outline falling and scraping along the rock face. The sunlight was all but gone. I didn't see where he fell, but I could hear the distant and sickening thud.

Me and Dufferin didn't speak for a minute or so. "We weren't here Chapman, just another accident or maybe a suicide." He patted the dirt off his trousers and swung his shotgun slightly as he talked. "Can I offer you some kind of reward?" He looked at me intensely.

"That's okay thanks, no. But I'm happy to go along with things," I answered, evenly. I turned and faced him and wrapped my coat a little tighter in the evening breeze. "Look, I don't know if your man Colrain was in on it too, heck even the local police, I'm not sure. So, I guess. I'm saying to play your cards pretty close about what you do next. I'll leave that up to you."

"I appreciate your candour, Mr. Chapman, and your advice, but yes, let me worry about that."

"One thing I ask, though, I don't want anything coming out about the affair."

He started to walk back towards the wall of the Causeway. "You have my word, Mr. Chapman."

"Considering the way things are, that will do just fine."

Chapter Forty-Four

The second knock on the door brought me to. I didn't know how long I had been gazing at the cursor on my computer screen. The room seemed darker and more silent if that's possible. I rubbed my hand over my face before standing. I had no idea what time it was or what to make of everything. I turned on a second table lamp and crossed the room to open the door.

The anxious face that greeted me was of a woman in her early forties, dark hair and light makeup. As I opened the door there was a flicker of relief present in her expression. The face was soft, altering the presence of a natural hardness. I didn't recognise her at all.

"Are you not going to ask me in?" she asked, with a tight smile.

I stepped back a step. "I'm sorry, can I help you?" I asked, "I hadn't ordered any room service."

Her face darkened and she blew out air. "For God's sake Billy," she said, pushing her way in past me. "Are you really that bad?"

I stared after her in some dismay, then slowly closed the door behind us. I wasn't quite in a full blown panic as yet, but my stomach was starting to jump around all over my body.

"I think you have the wrong room love, I'm sorry, but I don't know you," I said, trying to keep my shit together.

She fixed me a look and then shook her head at the ground before taking off her coat and throwing it on the bed. Something about that look was familiar. She walked slowly over to me, stood a foot away and spoke softly as if to a distressed child in the middle of the night. "It's me Billy. For God's sake, it's me! Mary, your wife, ex-wife."

I backed away and experienced an almost primal sense of danger.

"You're not my ex-wife. Look, I'm going to have to ask you to leave, I...."

"Billy, for fuck sake, we were married nine years," she shouted, and grabbed me all at once by my shirt and then paced backwards again, letting me go. Neither of us seemed to know how to stand or what to do next.

"Look," I said, still quite calmly. "I'm not this Billy of yours, my name is Brian Caskey and...."

"No it's not," she said, gently interrupting me again. "You're not well, Billy. We've been here before, it's just worse this time. God, much worse, what have you been up to... ay?"

She shook her hair from over eyes and cocked her head slightly to the left. I couldn't help but notice somewhere at the back of my mind that she was really quite pretty.

"I'm not called Billy," I said, feeling anger rising in me.

"Yes. That is who you are. You just don't want to be him anymore. You've created this other life, this pretend life. God, you've been running all over Belfast getting in all kinds of trouble."

"No!" I shouted. I felt almost all control had left me and I ran my hand through my hair and sat down on the edge of the bed. She stood around the other side, pacing. I longed for my medication, I hoped I was dreaming.

"Billy, we'll get you sorted. You're just not well. Dr. Colrain will get you back to your old self," she tried to say it soothingly, but failed. "I still care about you, everyone does. You wouldn't return my calls and I'm just so glad they rang me when you arrived here. I've not seen you since that wee stint you had in Knockbracken."

I was dumbfounded. Maggie. *Fuck, was I really losing it? My dead wife?* Or not dead. Maybe this was the hallucination now. This could be the psychosis. There was nothing else to do but try and get through it. I stood up and put all my will into controlling my voice,

"So, what am I supposed to believe? I'm not Brian Caskey? I know who I am… I'm an ex-police officer and I'm now a PI and I'm on an important case. Oh, yes, and my wife is dead by the way, blown up in a car bomb. So that can't be you. I don't know you."

She spoke softer still. "You were in the police, yes, but you left years ago. You were injured in a car bomb, not me. It affected you," she said, with a pained look. "We were together for years still after that. That's not what separated us. It was," she paused, awkwardly. "Something else. You're not a PI now, either. You were a freelance journalist for a few years and, well, the last few years you haven't been yourself. You had a lot to deal with. You haven't been well Billy."

"Billy?" I screamed, uncontrollably. "Who? Billy Chapman?"

"Yes, that's your name," she replied, evenly.

"The fuck it is. He's a character in a story that I invented. I created him!"

"You've created a lot of things, love, I'm sorry. You're confused, you're all mixed up. It's Brian Caskey who you made up. Please, let me call someone and we'll get you sorted out. Jesus, Billy, you've been all over the place accusing people of being drug dealers and what not and nearly getting yourself arrested."

I strode purposefully towards her around the bed, full of fear and rage.

"Why? Why would I do that? Huh? Tell me!"

"Don't you remember coming here?" she asked, reluctantly.

"Here? No, what do you mean?"

"You're so confused, Billy. You've been all over Belfast, Ards, even down to bloody Dublin, saying strange things to a lot of people and you're all mixed up love. You don't seem to remember some things and have invented others," she paused, and gathered herself up. "We came up here for a kind of holiday. It was two years ago. You were working on a missing person's story. A missing history student from Queens. You were writing a piece about it. We came here to stay while you were following up on leads."

I stared at her blankly. My world view was being sliced up in a bread cutter, into smaller pieces, with every new sentence.

She started to cry. "Don't you remember him?"

"Remember who?" I felt drawn to be closer to her and inched beside her onto the bed.

She opened her handbag and took out a tissue and dabbed at her eyes. She reached in again and lifted out her purse. She glanced up at me, questioning me or perhaps questioning herself. She flicked the clasp and lifted out a folded over photograph. She passed it to me. It was the boy with the football, standing in between the two Harland and Wolfe cranes.

"Our Sean," she said, with tears now cascading down her cheeks. "Can't you remember?"

I backed off the bed instinctively and almost fell to the floor. I felt as if I might lose consciousness and tried to keep myself from going under. I searched my mind as if trying to remember a dream from when I was a child. I looked at the photograph again and it looked strange, not less familiar, but different. I felt a pain in my stomach as if stabbed with something blunt.

"No," I said, to her and threw the picture onto the floor.

"Billy, please," she begged. "It was no one's fault, just a terrible accident. He fell, Billy, he fell.

My eyes blazed at her.

"No," I rasped, and left her to her quiet sobbing.

***

I fled the room and raced along the corridor and down the stairs. Outside would make everything okay, outside would have air and calmness and answers. I rushed through the now busy hallway and almost crashed straight into Loach. He looked the same as he was, or as I had imagined, or I don't know what. What I do know is I gave him a look as if he was Banquo's ghost. When I made it outside, crashing out of the porch, the rain was fierce and the wind unforgiving. It mocked my thin shirt and there was no respite here outside as I had imagined. I ran along the hotel's private path and out towards the cliff path. There was no one to be seen anywhere, or even for miles, as far as I could tell. A sheet of rain hung all around me like a broadsheet off an old printing press. I edged along the path towards the spot where Frank McKenzie would have fallen. I looked down to the rocks and the spray danced on the Causeway stones and the rain lashed against the cliff wall like a thousand bullets. I looked up to the sky and tried to release whatever it was I was keeping from myself. I closed my eyes and let myself go.

Chapter Forty-Five

I met with Loach at breakfast and savoured every piece of angina fuel knowing it would be my last Ulster fry up here. He took it well when I was honest and told him that I had to keep some of the whole truth from him. He seemed to accept that there were things I could not tell him for good reasons. I wanted to be straight with him about that. I said that McKenzie had fallen in an accident and that he had been being blackmailed, but that there were things I couldn't tell him and he couldn't say anything to anybody. He agreed and I knew he wouldn't break his word because he was a good man. I refused his offer of payment, but accepted the board and tram fare. I met Mary in the afternoon and I did tell her everything. She cried and I held her and we felt close to each other. We smoked a few cigarettes and then she walked me to the station. I didn't want to wait around and make things harder. The Causeway weather was more forgiving that day and it was a pleasant walk in even more pleasant company. She had thanked me earlier and I didn't care about that. What I cared about was that she was going to be okay. There wasn't much else for us to say to each other, but that was fine and it was comfortable. I felt a bit like Benandonner ripping up the Causeway behind me.

"See you in the funnies," she said.

About Simon Maltman

Simon Maltman is a writer and musician from Northern Ireland. This is his debut novel after previously having crime fiction short stories featured in a number of magazines and anthologies. He has also had poetry and articles published in a range of magazines. Simon has self-published a number of crime fiction e-books over the last year. There is work underway for further crime fiction releases in the near future.

Simon is an established musician, along with his current band The Hung Jury. He lives in County Down with his wife and two daughters.

Previous press for Simon Maltman:

"I'm amazed how a writer can cram so much into such a short space of narrative. You hit the ground running and it's a sprint finish."

Crime Book Junkie

"Praise Satan for Bangorian Simon Maltman."

Irish News

"Long may he continue."

Hotpress magazine

"A clever use of real photographs throughout brings an authentic feel to this compelling tale... a short but snappy read that gives a fresh glimpse into a life of crime and where it can lead you."

Writing.ie

"Those who foresaw the end of the book as artefact with the coming of the digital age hadn't banked on the ingenuity

and skill of a number of young writers who are converting the e-book into a work of artistic relevance. Such a case is that of Simon Maltman, a multifaceted writer and musician from Bangor."

Dr David M. Clark

Director Departamento de Filoloxía Inglesa

Universidade da Coruña

Social Media Links

Facebook:
https://www.facebook.com/simonmaltmancrimefiction

Facebook:
https://www.facebook.com/simonmaltmanandthehungjury

Acknowledgements

Thanks to my friends and family and in particular my harshest critic and editor- my wife Anna.

Gratitude to everyone who has taken the time to read my stories.

Big thank you to all at Solstice and those who have previously published my work.

Appreciation for the inspiration from Northern Ireland, it's a great place to live.

Special mention- thank you coffee!

If you enjoyed this story, check out the other Solstice Publishing books by Simon Maltman

Return Run

Professional thief Blake agrees to come in on a nightclub heist outside of Belfast. He doesn't count on a double cross or on stumbling on an old flame and a mess of murder and deceit. Blake was featured recently in the hardboiled story *Riot Score* and the press said:

"I'm amazed how a writer can cram so much into such a short space of narrative. You hit the ground running and it's a sprint finish."
Crime Book Junkie

and

"a short but snappy read that gives a fresh glimpse into a life of crime and where it can lead you."
Writing.ie

http://bookgoodies.com/a/B01I1Y6RX0

Let's Have Fun Vol 2

The longest day of the year brings fun, excitement, danger, and romance. Come along on a journey through the stories of ten talented authors as we celebrate Summer Solstice 2016. In this volume of Let's Have Fun, we explore this day in the far future, discover a crystal forest, and journey to past desire along with many more adventures.

Arthur Butt, Candace Sams, Chera Thompson, CS Patra, Dale S. Rogers, E.B. Sullivan, Ilena Holder, James Osborne, Lou Rera, Simon Maltman.

http://bookgoodies.com/a/B01HBSSTVK